The Passage of the Ruby Ring

PATRICIA LEWIS-BURRELL

ISBN 978-1-63885-749-5 (Paperback)
ISBN 978-1-63885-750-1 (Hardcover)
ISBN 978-1-63885-751-8 (Digital)

Covenant Books
11661 Hwy 707
Murrells Inlet, SC 29576
www.covenantbooks.com

This novel is dedicated to my brother, Donald "Donnie" R. Lewis, with love and affection.

Acknowledgments

I would like to acknowledge those who helped me through this exciting journey and process of *The Passage of the Ruby Ring*. This novel is rich in significance to me because I am a descendant of the Scottish Wardlaw clan, the inspiration for my story.

Therefore, I would like to especially acknowledge my precious mother, the late Ruth Emily Wardlaw Lewis, who was a direct descendant of Robert Wardlaw. Our ancestor, Robert Wardlaw, was born in Scotland on December 17, 1671, and died in Virginia (in the American Colonies) in 1725.

A sincere thank-you to my entire family. The love and support I have received from these wonderful cheerleaders is incredible! I love you all dearly.

I also would like to acknowledge Julie Wilson of the Abbeville Chamber of Commerce for information about the lovely town Abbeville located in South Carolina.

Thank you, Hannah Ray of the Abbeville Library, for directing me to the right place to answer my questions.

A warm thank you goes out to the Clan Wardlaw Association for their input on the Wardlaw history. Thank you, Mark Wardlaw and Diane Wardlaw.

A special thank you to my publication assistant, Kris Kempinski, who is absolutely wonderful and a complete joy to work with.

And of course, my publisher, Covenant Books, thank you; and I am truly grateful.

Wardlaw Clan Motto: *"Familias Firmas Pietas."* (Religion strengthens families.)
MacMillian Clan Motto: *"Miseris Succerrere Disco."* (I learn to succor the unfortunate.)

Catriona is pronounced as Cat-tree-oh-na.

Scottish Immigration to America after the Battle of Culloden in 1746 was significant. The Scots settled in all of the thirteen colonies but mainly in South Carolina and Virginia.

Prologue

The year was 1738, the weather was cold, and the threat of rain was in the air. Five-year-old Catriona's young body was starting to shake to warm her small frame against the cold while standing on the docks with her parents. Catriona's parents, Bain and Alana MacMillan, had purchased passage to the American colonies. Catriona's father, Bain, said sadly as he looked down at his precious daughter, "We are bound for a new adventure, Miss Cat"—a name he used often for his beautiful blue-eyed little girl. "We are leaving our beloved Scotland for a new home, but we will always be Scots." Catriona looked up at her father and smiled.

Little Catriona always thought her father was this sweet, huge man that she loved so much and always made her laugh, but today even at the tender age of five she knew her father was sad.

The voyage would take six weeks if the weather and wind was good; if not, it could take up to eight to twelve weeks. The survival statistics of young children making the voyage was not good, but Bain and Alana took solace in the fact that their child demonstrated a zest for life at such a young age.

Catriona's father picked her up in his strong arms as they boarded the ship. It started raining, and Catriona buried her face into her father's coat. She was frightened about the ship and the fact there was so many people. She felt safe in her father's arms. Bain, not wanting to let go of his daughter, had to in order to go over documents with the official. Bain sat Catriona down; her mother grabbed her little hand and brought her child close. Catriona just turned into her mother's skirts and held on.

There were mostly Scots on the ship that day, and amongst them was Robert Wardlaw with his wife and children. Robert Wardlaw was hoping this journey would be a new beginning for him and his family. Robert carried his youngest son, William, in his arms while trying to keep a tight hold on his wife, Jeanette, and older son, James, as the ship was leaving the Scottish harbor heading to the American colonies. A trip that would take months.

The Passage of the
Ruby Ring

Chapter 1

1747

Catriona MacMillan looked up at the clouds passing by and immediately thought they looked like a herd of sheep. She was lying on the ground in a field of wildflowers gazing up at the sky. It was quiet with a mild breeze blowing by; she was enjoying the solitude while watching the clouds create different scenes.

Catriona would sneak off to her favorite place to be alone for a moment, grabbing time for herself was near to impossible. As she watched the clouds float slowly by, she noticed one that looked remarkably like a ship. As Catriona watched the puffy white ship slowly move through the sky, it sparked a memory of the voyage with her parents from Scotland to the colonies. She pondered about the journey she made with her parents aboard the ship. Her memories of the voyage were scarce, but she did remember it was really long and smelled bad. She also remembered a horrible storm that, to this day, caused her to be afraid of lightning and thunder, and she did remember standing on the dock with her parents and her Papa picking her up and holding her close. Other than that, she didn't remember much of anything about the journey that took almost three months.

As fourteen-year-old Catriona lay peacefully in the field of wild flowers she thought she was alone, but she was not. Sixteen-year-old William Wardlaw was standing on a small hill looking out over the meadow when he noticed something move. When young William's curiosity got the best of him, causing him to take a closer look, he realized it was the MacMillan girl. This revelation caused a smile to come across William's face. He had known her as far back as he could remember and noticed her in the village. He also would see her at the church gathering once a month, but he had never really talked to her. One time he saw her, he remembered, it was her long red hair that could not be missed. William also remembered on that particular day she kept trying to put her bonnet on, but her hair kept falling out so she just tied the bonnet around her neck and let her hair fall down around her shoulders. To him, she was beautiful and had the bluest eyes he had ever seen.

William backed away from where he watched Catriona MacMillan lying in the wild flowers and went on his way to accomplish the task of gathering kindling for his mother.

As William walked home he thought about the valley where he saw the MacMillan girl. He knew the Wardlaw farm shared a border with the MacMillan's. William remembered his father saying that the MacMillans were good Scots. The field where Catriona MacMillan was lying in was actually split down the middle with MacMillan's owning half and the Wardlaw's owning the other. Young William laughed at this thought and wondered whose land she is really lying on.

Catriona knew she had to get up and go back to the cabin to help with the evening meal. She reluctantly rose, dusted herself off, and started her journey back to the little cabin where she lived with her parents and two brothers. As Catriona was walking home she glanced over at the Wardlaw's farm, she thought how much more room they must have compared to her family's cabin. It was evident their cabin was small in comparison to the Wardlaw's. This was probably the first time this actually crossed Catriona's mind that there was a difference. As she continued on her way, she remembered hearing her Papa say, "The little town of Brownsburg, where we shop, is actually located on Wardlaw property." Catriona was not a jealous or envious girl, she was sweet and kind, but she just needed space in her own little world at the moment and it was hard to find.

When Catriona got home she immediately went to work with her mother preparing the evening meal. Her eight-year-old brother, Camden, was with her father in the field. Camden was born in the colonies, and so was her youngest brother, Aiden, who was six. Six-year-old Aiden loved his sister Catriona and was her constant shadow. Both brothers looked up to their big sister with sincere affection. As the evening meal was being served into five dishes and then placed on the family table, Catriona's father and brother Camden came in with a clatter and fresh-washed faces with smiles. Catriona's father was exclaiming, "We are two hungry farmers, Mother!" then he kissed Catriona's mother on the cheek with such tenderness. Catriona had always known her parents loved each other, they would demonstrate it continually with kindness toward one another on a daily basis. That sweet kindness was also showered on their three children.

The five MacMillans bowed their heads while Catriona's father prayed for the good bounty that was before them. Catriona smiled as she watched her family as they gathered around the table eating their evening meal. She thought with a grateful heart, *We have so much love in this family.*

Catriona's father was excited about the yield he was expecting from his labors. Life was simple in the

MacMillan family; they all worked hard and always felt they were blessed. It had been a long and hard journey to get where they were today, but through the hardships, they were always thankful they had each other.

As Catriona and her mother were clearing the evening meal, the boys and her father went to the front stoop to relax, and her father would smoke his pipe. When the kitchen duties were finished, Catriona's mother called out for the boys to get ready for bed. Catriona went out to sit with her father in the coolness of the evening. She loved the smell of her father's tobacco almost as much as the wild flowers in the meadow. As Catriona and her father sat in silence that evening, Catriona wondered where her life would take her in this new world.

Little did she know that young William Wardlaw was thinking the same thing as he sat on his family's front porch that evening. William was wondering where his life would take him, but William also was thinking about Catriona MacMillan and was wondering what she was doing this evening.

William knew he would one day take a wife and be a farmer like his father and brother, but that day was a few years down the road. His brother James was getting married this fall to Elizabeth, and he was only nineteen. This new thought that had come to William's mind was a little unsettling. He abruptly stood up and thought, *This is way too much to think about at sixteen.* He headed to bed to rest his mind from his perplexing thoughts. As William laid his head down on his pillow, he thought, *I will get to see Catriona MacMillan at church on Sunday.* This thought brought a smile to young William as he drifted off to sleep.

The small log church located in the village was not only used for a church but also for other needs of the community. As William walked in with his family on Sunday he looked for the MacMillan clan. As he looked around the small church, he spotted Catriona. She was seated with her family. As he passed where she was sitting he held his hand out for Mr. MacMillan to shake and said good morning. Mr. MacMillan clasped down on William's hand with his calloused one and smiled as he said,

"Tis a fine day, young William." William answered Mr. MacMillan with, "Yes, sir, it is!" then took his seat with his family. Catriona saw William shake her father's hand and wondered why she had never really noticed William Wardlaw. He was a very nice-looking young man, she thought. When the service was over she smiled at young William as they walked out. William was in shock that she would smile at him, much less acknowledge him, and with a small delay he smiled back and said, "Good day, Miss Catriona." Catriona nodded. The small congregation dispersed for home and Sunday dinner.

Catriona thought about William for the next two days, and William also thought about Catriona. On the third day Catriona was outside bringing in laundry when William walked up and started talking to her father. She watched her father shake William's hand and then they both looked at Catriona. She thought, *What is going on?* As William started to leave he walked over to Catriona and said, "Good evening, Miss Catriona."

Catriona replied, "Good evening, Mr. William."

William stood there in one spot for a moment and then he said, "I asked your father if I could come to see you and sit for a while on Saturday evening." He continued, "Would you like that Miss Catriona?"

Catriona just stood there and stared at William. William thought she doesn't want to when Catriona suddenly blurted out, "Yes."

William smiled and said, "I will see you on Saturday." Catriona just looked at him and nodded. William turned to leave. And that was it. Catriona had a suitor, and she didn't have the faintest idea of what to do with him.

When Catriona walked back into the cabin her brothers were teasing her about having a beau; her mother shushed them out the door with a broom. Catriona just sat down at the table and looked at her mother with a look that was saying, "What do I do now?" Alana sat down and took Catriona's hand into hers and smiled. Alana questioned Catriona, "Do you like him, Catriona?"

Catriona replied to her mother, "I don't know. I do not really know him…I need to think about this."

Alana just patted her only daughter's hand and said, "You will know when you spend some time with him. You will like him or not." Alana stood up from her chair and walked outside to let her daughter think. As Alana stepped through the door, she smiled to herself and hoped that young William was a nice boy and would be kind and fair to her precious daughter.

Chapter 2

A few weeks after William Wardlaw asked Bain MacMillan if he could court his daughter, Bain fell off the roof of his cabin while patching a leak and broke his leg. Although it seemed like it was a clean break, this put Bain MacMillan out of commission for bringing in the harvest and storing for his family's food for the winter. The MacMillan family was worried about how they would manage while the head of their household was down with a broken leg. William stopped by the MacMillan farm to see Catriona on Sunday afternoon and also to offer his help after he heard at church what happened to Bain MacMillan.

Catriona, a bit distraught, told William that her Papa had fallen and broken his leg. She also told William that Dr. Angus McClendon set his leg and it was awful. Catriona nervously said to William, "We know we need Papa's help for the harvest. I am not sure what we will do." Catriona thought it was sweet when William told her father that he would help as much as he could with their harvest. Bain MacMillan was a proud man but grateful for William's offer.

The next morning the entire Wardlaw family showed up at the MacMillan farm to help bring in their harvest and storing. Bain MacMillan was touched by the Wardlaws' help and kindness, but he could not take any charity; that was the way of the Scots. Pride sometimes got in their way.

Bain MacMillan had but one valuable possession other than his family—a ruby ring. The ring was beautiful with the ruby set in the middle and small diamonds on each side. It was handed down from Bain's mother to him, and he had given the ring to Alana when he asked her to marry him.

Alana had always known she could only wear the ring on special occasions—as a farmer's wife, special occasions were far and few between to wear a ring so beautiful—so she put the ring in a safe place for keeping. Alana had said to Bain after she put the ring away, "The ring is too valuable to wear everyday as a farmer's wife. We should save it for a rainy day." While lying in the bed with a broken leg, Bain thought about what Alana had said a while back about the ring; he knew the rainy day was here. Bain asked Alana to fetch the ring. Alana brought Bain's mother's ring to him. He then asked Alana to go ask Robert Wardlaw if he could have a moment with him. Alana went to fetch Robert Wardlaw for Bain. She found him coming back from the field and asked him if he would have a moment with her husband. Robert Wardlaw followed Alana into the cabin to her husband's bedside. Bain held out his hand to Robert. Robert took Bain's hand. Bain said, "Robert, thank you for helping me and my family. I do not know if I can ever repay you."

Robert answered, "That is what neighbors do, Bain. We help each other."

Bain handed the precious ruby ring to Robert and said, "I want to give this to you for payment." Robert at first refused to take the ring, but knowing how proud he was himself, he knew it would be an insult not to take it from Bain, so he did reluctantly.

Bain MacMillan rested that evening knowing there would be food to eat for his family that winter. Robert Wardlaw put the ring up in a safe place when he got home and never spoke about it.

Bain MacMillan's leg healed, and by Christmas he had shed his crutch. As things got back to normal for the MacMillans, there was a budding romance between Catriona and William. Catriona looked forward to her Sunday afternoons with William, and sometimes during the week she would see him. Her affections were growing stronger for William Wardlaw, not just as a friend but something more. She was still young in mind and living totally in the present, but she knew she looked forward to seeing William and spending time with him. She wasn't actually thinking the same way William was at the moment; he was looking to the future, and that future included Catriona. William's feelings for

Catriona were developing at a fast pace and increasing every day; he now knew he loved her from the first time he saw her.

The following spring, Catriona turned fifteen, and William surprised her with a bouquet of wild flowers from her special place tied with a beautiful soft yellow ribbon for her hair. Catriona was touched by William's sweet actions, and she would always remember that was the day she knew she loved William Wardlaw with all her heart. As the days and months followed their love grew, and so did they. Catriona and William's love was strengthened by their kindness toward each other.

Two years later in the spring on her seventeenth birthday, William proposed to Catriona in her special place where the wild flowers grow. He got down on one knee and asked Catriona to marry him. She looked down at her precious William and said, "Of course I will, William. Yes, yes, I will marry you!" William placed Catriona's grandmother's beautiful ruby ring on her finger, kissed her hand, and told her he had loved her since the first day he met her. Catriona was so overwhelmed and surprised; she knew she loved William with all her heart. She reached down and took William's hand to her lips and softly kissed it. While tears rolled down Catriona's cheek, not only for the man she loved, but for her grandmother's ring on her finger. Catriona was grateful, she and her family thought her grandmother's ring was gone forever, but now it sparkled brightly on her finger.

William walked Catriona home, and as they approached the cabin, her entire family was sitting on the front porch her father built last season. Catriona announced that she was engaged, but everyone seemed to already know and were smiling. William shook Catriona's father's hand, and Catriona showed her father and mother her ring. They both were so excited for their one and only precious daughter. Anna hugged her daughter and kissed her on her cheek. Tears ran down Bain MacMillan's face; he just looked at William and nodded. William nodded back. That evening when Bain MacMillan said grace for their meal, he included William and his mother's ring returning to his family. There was a celebration not only in the MacMillan's home that evening but also at the Wardlaw's. William's parents were so excited for him and Catriona. They already loved Catriona and had fond feelings for her family. Robert Wardlaw looked at his wife and said, "This is a good match." They both agreed and were delighted for their youngest son, William.

For the last year William, his brother, and father had been building a cabin on his family's land. His father had given him some acreage like he did for his oldest son. When the cabin was finished, William proposed to Catriona. Catriona did not know anything about the cabin, and William wanted to make sure she said yes and would marry him before he told her.

A week after William proposed, he took Catriona to see their home. The cabin was precious with a small front porch. Catriona thought it was beautiful. It was so sweet with everything you needed, a present from William's parents. The fireplace was huge, and Catriona pictured herself sitting by the fire, all cozy, on a long winter night.

Catriona MacMillan and William Wardlaw were married in the fall of that year in 1750 after the harvest. It was a simple but sweet wedding with the two families and the minister. Catriona and William Wardlaw spent their first night together in their cabin close to Catriona's favorite place, the valley where the wild flowers grow.

The following morning after Catriona and William were married, Catriona sat on their little porch and thought with a smile, *This is where our lives will unfold.*

Chapter 3

1993

On Thursday afternoons, at precisely three o'clock, Katheryn Wardlaw Kensington would visit with her great-grandmother Emilia. Katheryn was in her last year of college majoring in history and currently working on a paper she was doing about her ancestral heritage. What started out as research for Katheryn's paper turned into a wonderful and exciting journey with her great-grandmother through the background of their family, especially the Wardlaw lineage.

The two—one graceful older woman with the knowledge of their family's history and one young woman eager for this knowledge—would sit together in the afternoons on Thursdays reliving the past.

Emilia Wardlaw Kensington was one of those gracious Southern ladies that believed, you should always have tea in the afternoon at precisely three o'clock. As Katheryn served the tea exactly as her great-grandmother had taught her on this particular Thursday, her great-grandmother Emilia asked, "My sweet Katheryn, have you ever been in love?"

Katheryn was somewhat taken back, she sat down and looked at the most precious person in her life. Katheryn smiled and answered, "I do not think so. I had a crush on a certain boy in high school, but to answer your question, Great-grandmother, I think not."

Emilia looked at her great-granddaughter with love and said, "My dear darling, you have something amazing to look forward to in your young life, and when it happens it will change your world."

Katheryn answered her great-grandmother with "I really have not met anyone that would be described as possibly changing my world yet, Great-grandmother."

The graceful Southern Emilia looked at her great-granddaughter with a smile and said, "Oh, my sweetheart, that day will come, and when you fall head over heels for this special young man, and he has to be special, always remember I told you this day would come."

Katheryn smiled and said with love, "You will be the first to know!"

Katheryn noticed there was a tiny metal box sitting on the table. She asked her great-grandmother about the tiny metal box. "What is this?"

Her great-grandmother answered, "Now, Katheryn, this is one of the most important stories in our family history I have to tell you. This story has been handed down through generation to generation. It is the story of the Scottish ruby ring and also about a great love story between Catriona MacMillan and William Wardlaw. They would be my great-times-six-grandparents and yours, Katheryn, would be, my, nine generations!"

Emilia Wardlaw Kensington continued to tell her story, "Catriona was only five years old when she sailed with her parents, Bain and Alana MacMillan, to the colonies from Scotland in 1738. Catriona grew into a beautiful young girl with striking red hair and the bluest of eyes. She met her husband, William Wardlaw, when she was a mere child, and they became the best of friends. Their parents settled in Brownsburg, Virginia, after coming to the colonies with many other Scots. They were all leaving Scotland during and before one of the most important battles, the Battle of Culloden in 1746, which changed some aspects of Scotland forever.

"Our ancestors, the Wardlaws and the MacMillans, were farmers, and their farms were adjacent to each other. At the time of the Revolutionary War and leading up to it, the Wardlaws migrated to the state of South Carolina in and around the town of Abbeville. And actually, the MacMillans followed. This is how we ended up in our lovely town of Abbeville. But, my dear Katheryn I am getting ahead of myself. Back to Catriona and William's story.

"Their love was pure, kind, and unselfish. Their lives were lived for each other. This tiny metal box once held the Scottish ruby ring that William Wardlaw gave Catriona MacMillan when he asked her to marry him. The ring was originally owned by Bain Wardlaw, given to him by his mother. When Bain fell and broke his leg and could not bring in the harvest for his family, the Wardlaw family helped. Bain gave the ring to Robert Wardlaw for payment, and when his son, William Wardlaw, asked Catriona MacMillan to marry him, he gave her the Scottish ruby ring. I guess it was just the right thing to do, giving the ring back to the family it originally belonged to!" exclaimed Great-Grandmother.

Katheryn looked lovingly at her great-grandmother and replied, "What a beautiful story." Katheryn opened the small fragile box, and it was empty. She looked at her great-grandmother and asked, "Where is the ring now?"

Her great-grandmother Emilia answered, "That story is for another day."

Katheryn knew her great-grandmother was getting tired, so all the questions running through her mind would have to wait for an answer at a later time. She gave her great-grandmother a kiss on the cheek and said, "I love you, and I will see you in a few days. This story of our family is so intriguing!"

There were sweet goodbyes, and as Katheryn got into her car to leave, she said out loud, "Wonder where the ring is?"

Chapter 4

1760

Life had been good to William and Catriona Wardlaw, and they were blessed with twin boys, Duncan and Callum, and a beautiful little girl named Aynsley, which meant "my meadow." Catriona thought that was a perfect name for her little girl as she was conceived at Catriona's favorite place in the meadow where the wild flowers grow. Catriona was outside with her children working in the garden. She had her five-year-old boys pulling weeds, and their older sister of eight was singing as she pulled carrots out of the rich dirt. Aynsley had a voice of an angel and loved to sing, especially to an audience.

As Catriona and her children were gathering their tools and baskets to head into the house to prepare the midday meal, a man came riding toward their home. As the rider came closer Catriona realized it was her younger brother, Aiden. Aiden yelled, "Catriona! Catriona! Papa is not well; it doesn't look good, Catriona, you need to come with me." Catriona quickly rounded up her children and told Aiden to hook up the wagon. She explained to her brother that William was not home so she would take the children to William's brother's, which was on the way to her parents'.

After leaving the children with her brother-in-law Catriona hurried to get to her parents' farm. As she approached her parents' home she was engulfed with gloom. Aiden was waiting for her as she pulled the wagon up to the house. Catriona looked at Aiden's face, and it spoke volumes to her; she knew the news was bad. Aiden helped her down from the wagon and said. "It doesn't look good, Catriona."

Catriona ran into the house and found her mother kneeling by her father's bed praying. Catriona knelt down beside her mother, put her arm around her frail shoulders, and prayed. Catriona felt Aiden's hand on her shoulder, and as she laid her hand on Aiden's, her father took his last breath.

A few days later at the funeral, as the preacher started to talk about the life of Bain MacMillan, Catriona's mind wandered back in time to the day she was on the dock in Scotland with her parents and her Papa scooping her up in his arms and how safe she felt. William squeezed Catriona's hand, which brought her mind back to what the preacher was saying about her Papa. "Bain MacMillan was a tower of a man, and his honesty was sometimes to a fault. He loved his family with all his heart, and his trust in God never wavered. He was a good neighbor and loved by many. Bain MacMillan will be sorely missed."

Catriona's mind raced with thoughts of sorrow as she looked at the grave that held her beloved father, then she looked at William and said, "I have never been this sad in my life. I am so concerned about

Mother now, knowing that Papa is not here to take care of her. My brothers and I will talk to Mother and hopefully come to a decision that would be best for her in the days to come." William put his arm around her. She looked into his comforting eyes and said, "How in the world would I ever get through this without you, my precious William?" William held her close. Catriona knew how much her Papa had loved William and respected him too. She knew William loved her Papa, especially when she saw tears rolling down her husband's cheeks when he found out her Papa had passed.

Catriona's heart was full of sadness, but what would make her move forward was the love for her mother, her brothers, and her family. She would always be grateful to her wonderful husband, William, for always being by her side. Catriona thought as she turned to leave the grave site, *I will always miss you, Papa. I love you.*

Chapter 5

Catriona stood in her favorite place, the meadow where the wild flowers grow, thanking God for her blessings. As she walked down through the meadow, she closed her eyes; her senses took over and seemed to get stronger with every step. She could feel the wind softly blowing by bringing the fragrance of the different flowers. She opened her eyes to all the beauty and color smiling with thankfulness, for her eyes to see, her nose to smell, and her ears to listen to the sounds of the valley.

Even though ten years had passed since the death of Bain MacMillan, Catriona's pain over the loss of her papa was still there. Although now, she could think of the precious moments she experienced with her papa, and she could even laugh at some of the stories the family told about him.

She reluctantly started back up the hill toward home when she saw maybe twenty riders along the ridge. She wondered who they were, but her thoughts quickly went back to enjoying the meadow and picking the beautiful wild flowers as she climbed the hill. By the time she reached the ridge, the riders were gone and she wondered again who they were.

When Catriona approached the cabin she saw her brothers, husband, and brother-in-law standing in a circle talking intensively. As she came within earshot she heard the men saying words like war, moving, and families. She walked up to the men and asked, "What is going on?"

All the men looked at her and then her husband, William, answered, "Just man talk, Catriona, nothing to worry your pretty little head about." Catriona shot a look at her husband, William, and he knew there would be a talk later for sure.

That evening after supper with the chores finished and the children put to bed, Catriona walked out on the porch where she found William in deep thought. She asked, "William, my pretty little head wants to know what is going on."

William asked Catriona to sit, then he took her hand in his and quietly said, "I am sorry for saying that, but, my love, you do have a pretty little head! There are some things going on in the colonies. There is talk about corruption within the colonial officials. Of course we already know this, but there is a movement starting to happen now. Hopefully this movement will have a positive impact with the colonial officials and they will be more equal and fair. There was a group of riders from North Carolina that came through today while you were taking your walk to the meadow. They brought news of a movement to fight for their rights. They asked us to join them."

Catriona immediately asked, "And what did you say, William?"

William looked at his beautiful wife with love, and he answered her question, "We told them we would support their efforts."

Catriona shot back a question, "What does that mean, William?"

William looked straight at his wife and said, "Catriona, I do not know if we will go down to fight with them or not, but we do support their efforts because we are still being ruled by England and the officials are corrupt! I do believe war is coming."

The two just sat and held hands; no more words were spoken that evening about war, but their thoughts were occupied with questions about what was to come and how it would affect their future.

Chapter 6

On May 16, 1771, in North Carolina, the Battle of Alamance was fought. The two opposing forces were colonial militia, under the command of Governor William Tryon, and a band of frontier citizens known as *regulators*, who raised arms against corrupt practices in local government.

Catriona and William, on a Sunday afternoon while gathered together for evening meal, were trying to explain to the twins that they were too young to go to war. The outbreaks of violence against the British in the Carolinas was escalating, and the twins wanted to be a part of the big war to come. Catriona said to her husband, William, "They are only sixteen. Please talk them out of this, husband." The thought of the twins leaving was so upsetting to Catriona; she had just got used to the idea of Aynsley being married and gone.

William spoke in a stern voice, "There will be no more talk of war today! You are upsetting your mother!"

Both young men said, "Yes, sir." Of course, William knew this would not be the last of it. He knew his boys were itching to leave and go down to South Carolina. He wanted to at least keep them with him for one more year. Deep down everyone knew this war for independence would happen and was actually already being fought.

Aynsley and Robert Finley were married a year ago, and they were now settled in a little township called Abbeville in South Carolina. The couple met when Robert and his family were traveling through on their way to South Carolina and stopped to visit with the Wardlaws. The two families had known each other before in Scotland.

When Aynsley and Robert met for the first time, Robert Finley declared to himself, "I will marry her someday, for she is the most beautiful lass I have ever seen." Aynsley was also immediately smitten with young Robert Finley, and six weeks after they met they were married.

It had been very lonely for the entire Wardlaw family after Aynsley left; they all missed her and all had a longing in their hearts to see her, for she was a spirit to behold. Aynsley's love for her family radiated from her, and you could feel it as she walked into a room. She had been and still was a complete joy, a gift to all.

The twins looked forward to seeing their sister again and was hoping it would be soon rather than later. The boys knew deep down leaving their father's farm would be hard on their parents. The idea of them leaving was, in reality, a hard decision for both. Their youthful minds looked at war as being involved in a movement of excitement and glory. They never thought about the other side of the coin, which included taking a life or giving theirs. They would fight one day, but both young men would look back at an easier time of living on the farm with their parents, with wistful thoughts.

Catriona's brothers ran their mother and father's farm. Their mother had stayed in her home and was happy there at this time. The brothers were both married and had children of their own now. They had built homes for their families, and Mother was in the middle. Someone was always checking in with her and taking care of her needs. Sometimes she would come and stay a while with Catriona but would always want to go back to her little cabin to be close to her husband whom she dearly loved and missed.

One day as Catriona was working in her garden, she thought her world would be complete if she could see her precious daughter, Aynsley. She missed Aynsley and longed to see her again. She hoped one day soon she would be able to go visit her daughter, who was also her friend. As the tears rolled down Catriona's cheeks, she asked God to please keep Aynsley in his care.

Chapter 7

The years seemed to fly by since the last time Catriona heard Aynsley's beautiful voice; she missed her daughter, and the ache in her heart for her was constantly there.

The war was raging, and the boys had left last year for Abbeville, South Carolina. Catriona could not shake her sadness, and William knew this, because he also had an ache in his heart for their children. Catriona was looking through her treasures she kept in a box hidden under their bed. Locks of hair from her children, sweet notes from William, pressed flowers, and a little box that held her engagement ring. She opened the little box and gazed at the beautiful ruby ring that once belonged to her grandmother, her father's mum. She lovingly put all her treasures back into the box and returned the box back to its hiding place. William was standing at the door watching his lovely wife as she stood up from hiding her treasurers. He smiled at her and she smiled back; he knew she was saddened about not being able to see their children. William opened his arms, and Catriona went to her husband. She felt his arms surround her as she embraced him. William softly spoke. "My love, we will go see the children, this I promise you."

Catriona looked up into her husband's eyes and said, "I love you, William Wardlaw."

William looked down at his wife and said, "I love you too, sweetheart."

After harvest that year William and Catriona set out on their journey to South Carolina, not knowing exactly how long the trip would take but hoping they would be there by Christmas. They rode on horseback packing lightly but carrying what they needed for protection. The great wagon trail was not always easy especially at this time of year, so they decided to go on horseback. Also, this way they could hopefully avoid any fighting between the British and the rebels.

The journey would be hard and sometimes dangerous, but Catriona was determined to see her children. She felt a calmness knowing that her and William's trust in God was rooted and solid. Every day and night Catriona and William would pray for safety and for God to watch over them. God answered their prayers and guided them on safe paths that held not only safety but clean water and food. They estimated it would take them around twenty-five days to get to Abbeville, but in reality, it took thirty-nine days to reach their destination.

Tired, dirty, and weary Catriona and William rode into Abbeville two days before Christmas; the year was 1774. They navigated the township to find their daughter's farm. When they arrived at Aynsley's home, it was not a farm but a wonderful home within the town limits. William walked up to the front door and knocked. The door opened, and a small child looked up and said in the most precious little voice, "Hello, may I help you?" A young woman stepped into view and pulled the child back. William asked if it was the Finley residence, and the young woman's eyes grew wide, and she screamed, "Pa!" and grabbed her father. Aynsley said, "Oh, Pa, I never thought I would see you and Mum again!" Then she spotted her mother and squealed in excitement, threw her arms around her mother, and they both held on to each other and wept. It was a wonderful reunion. Aynsley announced to her parents, "Meet your grandchild, Catriona."

William and Catriona's first grandchild named after her grandmother. Catriona was so moved that Aynsley would name her daughter after her. The child looked just like her mother with beautiful red curls surrounding her pretty face. William said to little Catriona, "Hello, it is so nice to meet you, granddaughter."

Little Catriona looked up at her grandparents with a big smile and said, "Hello."

Catriona said to Aynsley, "She is just like you as a child!"

Catriona asked her daughter, "Do you have any news about your brothers?"

Aynsley answered, "I have some, not sure how old the news is though. Last thing I heard was they both were in Charleston and well." Catriona squeezed William's hand as they both looked into each other's eyes.

William said, "Maybe we will hear some more news soon."

"Oh, I am sure we will, but they are safe and working with Robert and his father," Aynsley added. Catriona and William smiled at each other with the knowledge knowing that the twins were safe.

Aynsley's house was so beautiful and stately, Catriona thought as she walked through. The room alone given to Catriona and her husband, William, was almost as large as their cabin back home and it had a lovely sitting area. Catriona raised her arms, looked all around the room, then looked at her precious daughter and asked, "Aynsley, where did this all come from?"

Aynsley answered, "Scottish wealth, Mum." Aynsley continued to say, "Evidently the Finleys were quite well-off before they came to the colonies, but I think the bulk of their fortune was inherited from Robert's mother, the English side of her family, and I was told it was huge!" She went on to say, "They were in a covered wagon, Mum. I would not have ever guessed they were wealthy! But I do know one thing, I would have loved Robert Finley no matter if he was penniless!"

Later that afternoon, Catriona noticed that Ansley had servants in the kitchen and on the property that adjoined Robert's parents. Aynsley's husband was a lawyer as well as his father. Both gentlemen were working in Charleston on a project with a man and his son called Thomas Pinckney. To say the least, William and Catriona were impressed. They both conveyed this to their daughter.

Aynsley announced to her parents that they might have two aspiring young lawyers their selves; Duncan and Callum both had been taken under her father-in-law's wing. William and Catriona were amazed, and both said, "You should have told us that first!"

Aynsley answered, "I am so sorry, just with all the excitement." About that time, little Catriona walked into the sitting room while rubbing her sleepy after nap eyes. What a joy it was to see her granddaughter, Catriona thought, and to see her beautiful daughter, her beautiful home, and hear news of the twins. Catriona and William's hearts were full and thankful.

That night, kneeling by the bed that was absolutely wonderful, Catriona and William prayed together, thanking the Lord for their safe journey and finding Aynsley, meeting their first grandchild, little Catriona, and hearing news of the boys. They also prayed for those left behind, Catriona's family as well as William's. As Catriona and William got into the bed they said another prayer for the most wonderful bed in the world, and they laughed, held each other, and drifted off to a deep sleep.

The next morning, there was an array of activity; with Christmas one day away there was much preparation to do in Aynsley's household. This Christmas Eve, Catriona and William were so thankful to be able to spend it with their daughter and granddaughter. Later that day they were having tea and biscuits in the parlor when all of sudden the front door burst open and three young men were singing in harmony, "Happy Christmas, Catriona and Aynsley!" William and Catriona got up and walked into the foyer to see what was going on. Aynsley was coming down the stairs with little Catriona, and they all met up in a flurry of hugs, questions, and sheer happiness. The three young men were Duncan and Callum, the twins, and Robert, Aynsley's husband. What a reunion the family had that evening catching up with news about them, the war, their lives, and accomplishments. The twins indeed were studying the law under Robert and his father's guidance. Catriona looked at her boys and thought they have become handsome young men and she noticed they were dressed in gentlemen's clothing. She was so proud. William's heart was bursting with pride as he watched his children. Catriona couldn't help thinking how in the world could she leave these people, her people. William thought this would be the best Christmas they had ever had.

Robert was completely and totally the best host, husband, and father. William and Catriona were so happy to see Aynsley and Robert's love for each other play out in so many ways. William thought as he watched the family, *It gives you a wonderful feeling to know your children are happy and loved.* This is what Catriona and William saw every time they looked at Aynsley, her husband, and the twins. Happiness and love.

Robert's parents joined them for the Christmas meal, and Catriona remembered how nice they were when she had met them before. The boys and Robert were to leave and go back to Charleston after the New Year's. Catriona savored every moment she could spend with them. They were studying and working on big things to come, they both said.

After New Year's, Duncan, Callum, and Robert made their journey back to Charleston. Mr. Finley would follow them in a few days. Mr. Finley approached William about a farm that needed watching over and asked if he would take a ride with him to check on it. Mr. Finley told William that the farm had been his brother's and was quite profitable and that his brother had left to go back to England with his wife's family. Mr. Finley did not think his brother would return and had left the property in his hands to do what he thought was best.

William and Mr. Finley rode out to the farm to look it over. William's first thought was a question as he approached the farm, *This place is beautiful, how could someone leave it?* The lane to the house was imposing with beautiful oak trees lining it. As William and Mr. Finley talked riding up to the house, William found out that the farm acreage was not as large as his in Virginia, but the house was finer. The barn was bigger and the garden was much larger. As they walked into the house William thought it was a much larger version of his parents' home and he knew Catriona would really like this house. As they toured the property William told Mr. Finley that it was a fine piece of land and he should get a good price. Mr. Finley said there was no one to buy; with the war and his involvement in Charleston, he was afraid it would fall to ruin. William said, "Maybe your brother will be back one day."

Mr. Finley sadly said, "That would not be possible. My brother is sick, and I am afraid I will never see him in this world again."

William said, "I am sorry to hear that, John."

John Finley answered, "Thank you, William."

The two men rode back into town, and both were thinking the same thing but did not say a word out loud. That night William told Catriona about the farm and John Finley's brother. Catriona was saddened to hear about John's brother's illness. In their prayers that evening, John Finley's brother was included.

Chapter 8

Two weeks passed and William was getting things ready to make their journey home. He needed to make arrangements for a wagon, thinking it would be easier on Catriona when they made their journey back to Virginia. He stopped in at the blacksmiths to talk to him about his needs. There was a familiar man talking to the blacksmith about a new shoe for his horse, and then he asked about the Wardlaws. William spoke up and said, "I am William Wardlaw."

The man answered, "Then you are the man I am looking for. I have a letter for you from your family. My name is Paden Gregor. My family lived on a farm not too far from your father's." William immediately recognized Paden, but he had not seen him for several years and in that time the young boy had grown into a young man. William shook hands with Paden and gave him a pat on the shoulder. Paden looked at William with sadness, but William took it for weariness from his trip. After Paden finished his business with the blacksmith he reached into his saddlebag for the letter. William took the letter and thanked Paden for bringing it to him. Paden said, "Was coming this way, glad to do it." William excused himself and walked outside to read the letter. As William opened it he knew immediately it was from his father.

November 28, 1774

Dear son and family,

I sincerely hope this letter gets to you and finds you and your family well. I have good news and bad. Bad first. The colonial militia have confiscated your property; your brothers and I think mine will be next. So far they have left Catriona's mother and brothers alone, but I fear it is not long before they will. We have all talked, Catriona's family as well as ours. We are heading your way in hopes of finding somewhere to live. It is heartbreaking, and I am so glad you and Catriona are not here. I am sorry, son. We love you and hopefully will see you soon.

Your father,
Robert Wardlaw

William just stood there and looked at the letter in disbelief. His farm, his parents, their entire family has been affected. As William stood there in disbelief Paden Gregor walked up and said, "I am sorry, William. The same thing is happening all over the valley."

The two stood quietly for a moment, then William looked at Paden and said, "God will see us through this and the British be damned."

As William was leaving he told Paden to take care and asked him if he wanted a good meal, to please to come to supper tonight at his daughter's. Paden gratefully accepted and said he would be there.

All William wanted at the present was to see Catriona, and when he got to his daughter's home he was frantic. Catriona was in the garden with their granddaughter; she looked up and saw her husband with a disturbing look on his face. Catriona asked with concern, "William, what is wrong?"

William said, "I need to speak to you in private."

Catriona said, "Okay." She sent her granddaughter into the house with a small basket of vegetables.

William took her by the hand and said, "We need to go to our room. I have news from home."

Catriona was full of questions as they walked in and up the stairs to their room. Catriona asked, "William, what is going on?" As William closed the door he handed the letter to Catriona. She opened the letter, and as she read she had to sit down. Catriona asked in a concerned voice, "What will they do?" When Catriona finished the letter, she looked at her precious husband and asked, "What now, my dear husband?"

At the moment William had no answers. They sat and held each other. All they had and worked for was now in the hands of the colonial militia, which represented the British Crown. After a long silence William spoke, "We will find a way to receive our families and pray they make it safely here." William's mind was racing to find a solution. William told Catriona he needed to go to Charleston to see John Finley. Catriona didn't ask any questions; she trusted her husband and preceded to help William pack for his journey to Charleston. She went down to the kitchen to get the cook to make him something to eat and also food to take with him.

Aynsley walked into the kitchen to find her mother with a serious look on her face and asked her mother with concern, "What is it?" Catriona told her daughter that she would explain, but right now she had to help her father. William walked into the kitchen to find his wife and daughter. He said he was ready; he kissed his wife and left.

Catriona sat down with Aynsley and explained everything. Aynsley was astonished with the news. "How could this happen to our family, Mum? How awful for all of them," Aynsley asked with an uneasiness. They just sat and thought about how horrible it must be for their family. Catriona was concerned about her mother and how she would be on the trip; it was long and hazardous. She prayed for safety for her family and William's trip to Charleston. She would be glad when this was over and everyone was safe.

Chapter 9

The trip took William nine days to get to Charleston. He arrived midday and immediately went to find John Finley. He knew John was working with several people at the Pinckney Law Office. William found the law office and was met at the door by a large armed man. Questions immediately started rising in William's mind. William introduced himself to the large armed man and asked to see John Finley. The man at the door reluctantly answered William with "Just one minute" and shut the door.

William was confused. After a few moments, the door opened, and he was asked to come in. William was led into a small waiting room and was asked to take a seat. Still more confused he waited, and after about ten minutes John Finley opened a door that was connected to the waiting room and said, "William, what a nice surprise! Please come into my office."

William followed John Finley to his office. As he walked behind John down a long hall, he could hear many voices coming from another room. When they reached John's office the two sat down, and William preceded to tell John what had happened in Virginia. Then he asked if he could buy John's brother's place. William continued to tell John that this would help him to have a place to start from when the family arrived. John Finley declared, "Absolutely, William! I will draw the papers up immediately, and we can sign them when I come home in a few weeks."

William was thankful and relieved. William asked John to see the boys before he left to go back and also about the man at the front entrance. John

Finley said in a quiet voice, "The man at the front door is for protection from people we will not mention, but they come from a different country with a wink. William, I cannot tell you what we are doing here, but I can tell you it is for the betterment of our soon, hopefully, country. Your boys are safe, and I would lay down my life for them. You have my promise. There is fighting going on, but they are, what you would say, undercover. It would be better to see them at another time. If you like I will give them a letter or a message. Actually, a verbal message would be better." William asked when the boys would be back in Abbeville, and John told him in a few weeks. William said it would keep.

William reluctantly left and headed home without seeing the boys. William was still confused, but he figured he had more knowledge today after he spoke with John Finley than when he first found out they were working on a project in Charleston. He knew now they were working on something that concerned the colonies. He looked around and saw red coats everywhere. William prayed for the safety of the twins and his and Catriona's families as he headed back to Abbeville.

When William arrived back at his daughter's, he sat down with Catriona and Aynsley and explained to them his plans. He and Catriona would move immediately to the farm and start getting everything ready to receive the family. The place was already furnished, so they would not need much.

So the plans were in place, and after a good night's sleep William and Catriona moved into their new home. They cleaned and Aynsley brought help and before you knew it there was a cozy fire in fireplaces and food cooking in the kitchen. William looked at Catriona lovingly and said, "We are home, sweetheart."

She smiled and sweetly answered, "I love you, William Wardlaw."

William smiled as he said, "I love you too, my dear wife."

In the following days William purchased extra livestock for what lay ahead for the families. The farm had horses, wagons, and chickens; it was well-stocked, and even the pond was full of fish.

John Finley had hired a man to feed the livestock and watch over the place since his brother left. William kept him on; he seemed like a good fellow. He was an older gentleman alone in the world, so William asked him to please stay, and he said he would and was thankful. So Mr. Glen became part of the family.

After a few weeks William and Catriona had settled in nicely and could not believe they lived in this beautiful home. John Finley, Robert, and the twins came home, all with great enthusiasm.

The twins arrived at their parents' new home with excitement knowing their parents would be living in Abbeville. Duncan and Callum were different, Catriona observed; she thought more polished maybe. She was overwhelmed with pride watching their interaction with their father. She knew they had grown in ways that would not have happened on the farm in Virginia. She knew God had a plan for her family, and she was able to watch it firsthand! Catriona was so incredibly grateful to have her children close again.

Duncan and Callum were upset to learn of the news from Virginia, knowing their families had been and were still in harm's way. Callum announced, "The future holds promise for the colonies, a good future, and we are all a part of it! This is a dangerous time but also an exciting time."

Duncan added, "True, brother, but that is all we can say at the moment." Callum nodded to his brother, and a silent understanding passed through both young men.

Callum asked his father when he thought the family would arrive. William answered his son, "I calculate somewhere around mid-March but could be sooner. They are traveling through snow and cold weather, so I really think mid-March."

Duncan said with concern, "I will be glad when they get here." Everyone concurred.

The next day John Finley dropped by with the papers for William to sign. Both men went into a small parlor that had a desk and two chairs for William's use. William closed the door. Both men sat down, and as William was looking over the papers, he stopped and looked at John and said, "I can't sign this, John, this is not fair to you and your brother!"

John Finley answered, "This is what my brother wanted, William."

William replied, "I just don't know what to say."

John said, "There is nothing to say but this. I say thank you for taking over this farm! Now, William, sign please."

William signed the papers, handed them to John with a handshake and a "God bless you, John Finley."

John Finley replied, "God bless you, William Wardlaw."

The two men joined the others, and William gave Catriona a wink. She knew immediately that things were finished and the farm now belong to them.

That night, William and Catriona knelt and prayed and thanked God for providing a place for them and their families. The home would, from that day forward be called The Wardlaw House.

Chapter 10

Mid-March came and went; they were now looking at the end of March for the family to arrive. William and Catriona tried not to worry, but the anticipation was written all over their faces.

It was now going into the second week of April with no arrival of family and no word. William decided to ride out to see if he could at least find some news or the families. As he was saddling his horse in the stable he heard a loud noise and ran out to see what it was; it was four wagons coming down the road to the house. Tears ran down his cheeks. Catriona ran out the front door to William. They both were crying with joy; their prayers had been answered.

William helped his mother down and just held her. His father came around and hugged them both. The reunion was unexplainable. Catriona and her brothers were in the midst of a happy flurry. William watched as Catriona slowly slumped to the ground and ran to see what was wrong. Camden, Catriona's brother, said to William, "Mother did not make it." Catriona was inconsolable. Camden and William helped her up and walked her to the front porch to sit. Someone brought her a cup of water. She just sat, and the tears rolled down her cheeks as she watched the activity—unloading and wagons being moved to the barn area, horses unhitched and taken care of, the children exploring and laughing. Catriona wondered why they were so happy when she just found out her mother was gone.

Catriona was in shock, and her thoughts were not clear. That evening she asked Camden if he got the box from under her bed. She had told him before she and William left, if anything happened, to please get the box from under her bed. Camden looked at his sister with sincere love and said softly, "My sweet sister, no, I did not. It was gone when they let me go in to look. All I found was a small metal box. I am so sorry, Catriona."

Catriona looked at William and then just fainted. William carried her to their room and laid her gently on the bed. He sat with her until she aroused and never let her hand go. Catriona had a hard time focusing, but after a short while all things came clear. She looked at her husband with teary eyes and said, "Oh, William, my ring is gone, and so is my mother."

William said, "I know, my love."

He held her close through the rest of the night. He knew her grieving for the loss of her mother would take time. William prayed for Catriona and thanked God for delivering the rest of the family safely. William took a deep breath and thought, *No matter what happens, now we are all together. Wardlaw House and Abbeville is now our home.*

Chapter 11

1994

Katheryn Wardlaw Kensington was getting ready to graduate from college in two days. This was the best year of college, Katheryn thought, because it had included spending so much time with her great-grandmother Emilia Wardlaw Kensington. Her major paper had been a wonderful journey down through the history of her family told by her sweet great-grandmother. Great-grandmother explained about the trials, hardships, and especially love of their family. The memories told by her great-grandmother were nothing short of the makings of a wonderful novel. The only thought that kept nagging Katheryn was what happened to the ruby ring. Between her great-grandmother and a monumental extensive amount of research, Katheryn had narrowed it down to two names in charge at that particular time in that particular area in history. She also narrowed it down to certain names that served under these individuals. She knew it could take a lifetime to get a good lead and maybe even more time than that, but she was determined to give it a shot. Katheryn planned to tour Europe after graduation, but her great-grandmother changed her mind; instead she decided to study at Oxford for her master's. Katheryn thought this was logical, and while she studied she could continue to look for the ring and the man who took it. She applied at Oxford and was accepted. Great-grandmother was so excited because this was her idea, and she insisted paying Katheryn's entire way. Katheryn thought, *How could you turn that offer down!* Great-grandmother even added it to her will in case something happened to her. Katheryn loved her great-grandmother dearly. She also admired her, Emilia Wardlaw Kensington was all the charm and grace of the past, present, and future all wrapped up in one beautiful very special lady.

Three days after graduation Katheryn boarded a plane at Greenville-Spartanburg Airport bound for England. She would spend a few days in London and then travel by train to Oxford. She already had an apartment near the University, and she would obtain a car once she was settled. Driving on the wrong side of the road and on the wrong side of the car might be a challenge, but she thought, *I can do this*. As Katheryn laid back in her seat, wrapped the blanket over her, and listened to the roar of the plane, she drifted off to sleep dreaming about the adventures to come and Oxford.

Katheryn's plane landed in London at Gatwick International Airport at 8:10 a.m. She glanced down at her watch noticing that at home it was 3:10 a.m., thinking today is going to be a long day. After getting through customs, which seemed like a lifetime, she gathered her luggage and looked for the Gatwick Express Train that would take her to Central London. After finding her way to the Gatwick Express she boarded the train, stored her luggage, and sat down with a sigh; it was now 10:45 a.m. London time. Katheryn watched from her window seat as the train pulled out heading for Victoria Station, Central London. She was tired, but her excitement dominated as she looked at the beautiful landscapes and quaint neighborhoods with small manicured lawns and fields with boarders made from shrubs. Katheryn thought how lovely it was, and she couldn't wait to explore.

The train arrived at Victoria Station at 12:15 p.m., London time. Katheryn gathered her things then grabbed her luggage. When she walked out of the station she was met with a flurry of activity. It was a sunny day, and she was looking in her bag for her sunglasses. After she put her glasses on she looked around in amazement. London reminded her of New York City but with shorter older buildings. She noticed the architecture of the station, and the surrounding buildings were stunning. She hailed a cab, an educated accomplishment she learned to do while visiting her uncle and aunt in New York growing up. Katheryn smiled when the black cab pulled over to pick her up and thought, *This shiny cab looks like it came right out of a 1940s movie.* She hopped in with luggage in tow and gave the driver her address, then she sat back to take in the sights. Katheryn's first thought while riding in the cab through the city was, *I think I am really going to like London.*

After checking in her hotel, which was absolutely lovely (the one Great-grandmother insisted on), she decided to put her watch on London time and get something to eat. It was almost two thirty in the afternoon, and she was famished. She walked a short distance and found a place that was still serving. She walked in and ordered fish and chips because that was all they served. There was no place to sit and eat; she walked outside and spotted a bench a couple of stores down. She walked down to the bench and sat down. She opened her slightly cool beverage and pulled back the wrapper surrounding the fish and chips. The first bite of the fish she would remember for the rest of her life. Katheryn thought the fish was the best she had ever had and the chips doused with vinegar was wonderful. She would always remember her first meal in England with fondness. After she ate she went back to the hotel and slept until the next morning.

The next morning Katheryn showered and got ready for the day. Picking out something light to wear, she hurried downstairs for the breakfast that was served exactly from six until nine in the morning. Her timing was great; it was eight o'clock. She ordered and decided to have tea with her meal. She loved coffee in the morning, but she decided to "do as the Romans do" and have tea. The tea was wonderful, and her breakfast was interesting. Eggs good, bacon thick as ham but really good, the pork and beans were a little odd for breakfast, but she ate them anyway because she was so hungry and as it turned out they were good too.

After breakfast she rushed back up to her room and grabbed her backpack, shoved a jacket in it in case she met cooler weather, and hit the street. The day was beautiful, sun shining and people moving in every direction. It was great. She looked at her map and decided her first stop would be the famous statue of Queen Victoria's husband, Prince Albert of

Saxe-Coburg. The statue was very large in fact much larger that Katheryn had expected. Katheryn read from her London travel book, the Albert Memorial in Kensington Gardens is one of London's most ornate monuments. It commemorates the death of Prince Albert in 1861 of typhoid.

She stayed for a while to study the intricacies of the memorial. Katheryn thought as she looked up at the statue of Albert, Victoria must have loved him very much.

She noticed one of those red two decker buses riding by and stopping not too far away. She headed toward the bus parked at a load and unload point, bought a ticket and hopped on. Katheryn found a seat on top and sat back and relaxed to watched the view. She thought London was so manicured and clean. She passed the corner famously known as Speaker's Corner. She was having fun seeing all the places she had read about. Katheryn wanted to make the most out of the time she had today because she would leave tomorrow for Oxford. She had appointments not only in a few days at the university, but she also wanted to secure her apartment and get everything she might need before she had her Oxford appointments. They were passing the famous department store Harrods. Katheryn was making mental notes of what she wanted to do when she came back to London from Oxford. Then they rode through Piccadilly Circus; she dotted that down. The National Gallery was a must-stop and, of course, Westminster Abbey. She was so excited she got to see Buckingham Palace when they were having the changing of the guard. The formality was awesome, colorful and full of pomp and circumstance. *Very Royal,* Katheryn thought.

The small shops and pubs caught Katheryn's eye. She hopped off and went into a pub for some lunch. She found out quickly that you have to order at the counter first. She ordered a bowl of soup and tea. When she tasted the first spoonful of the soup, she thought she was in heaven; it was delicious, the bread was scrumptious, and of course you had to slather butter all over it to have the true taste. After lunch she just walked, looking and taking in the sights and people. London was unique, like New

York City, but London, like New York, had its own personality.

Katheryn thought, *I am going to really enjoy this journey Great-grandmother has sent me on.*

Chapter 12

The train ride from London to Oxford was just long enough to catch a quick nap. Katheryn's jet lag was finally catching up with her, but she kept trying to convince herself she was adjusting quite well. The nap she wanted to take was to no avail—too much to see and of course they had a baby on board that was not happy at all.

Katheryn arrived in Oxford and was moved by its entirety, the complete essence of learning. It was beautiful, the oldest university in the English-speaking world she read from her travel book, and was imposing, to say the least she thought.

She found her flat located near the university. Katheryn dragged her luggage up two flights of stairs to her floor and in the process almost knocked a guy to his knees. The poor guy was a young Englishman and he offered to help Katheryn and she gladly accepted. She introduced herself, and so did he. Then he called her a "yank." Katheryn explained she was not a yank. She was from South Carolina, which was located in the southern part of the country. "Yanks," she said as she was laughing, "are from the North, but I guess you guys refer to all of us Americans as yanks."

The young Englishman smiled and said, "We do."

They both laughed, and he said in his English accent, "I am also from the South."

Katheryn laughed at the young gentleman. When she found her door, she found her key and opened the door and was astonished! The flat was mostly windows and bright and sunny, Katheryn said, "This is really a bright place!" Her new friend, Oliver Middleton, walked over to a pole of some sorts and started cranking, which caused a cover to cross over the windows. Katheryn was laughing and telling Oliver, "You are a lifesaver!" Oliver smiled and asked if there was anything else he could help her with. Katheryn thanked him and said, "No, you have been great." Oliver excused himself and left his phone number in case she needed to ask anything and let himself out.

Katheryn began to nest and make a list as she went. After she put everything in a place she grabbed her list and headed out to find a market. She found one barely two blocks from her apartment.

As Katheryn headed back to her apartment, she thought, *I have purchased too much! What was I thinking?* Now she was looking at making two flights of stairs with all she had in her arms. She decided she would have to make two trips. As she walked up to her building three people came out a door on the bottom floor. Katheryn looked up and saw a sign that said, "Lift." With a huge smile on her face she went through the door and found the lift. It was small, really small, but adequate. She rode the small lift to her floor and wondered why Oliver didn't tell her about the elevator. It was probably because she was already a few steps from the second floor when Oliver offered to help. Katheryn was very excited to have discovered the lift. The lift was small, but in her mind it was the best thing since sliced bread!

Over the next several weeks Katheryn explored and accomplished everything she needed for her classes, which started in two weeks. The Fourth of July was the first thing she experienced in England that made her homesick. She missed the celebration, the gathering of family, and the food—oh, how she missed the food. She had brought a small American flag with her and placed it in a special place in her apartment. On the Fourth of July, she called Grand, which made her homesick even more, so she decided ice cream would be the remedy for her mood.

As Katheryn walked to the ice cream shop three blocks from her apartment, she saw Oliver sitting with a very attractive girl on a bench in this beautiful little park. Katheryn had noticed these small attractive parks were scattered all across the university. She looked at Oliver and his friend; she quickly noticed they really seemed to be into each other. Katheryn smiled as she thought, *That is why I hav-*

en't seen much of him, and when I do it was only in passing. She finally arrived at the ice cream shop, and now was the moment of decision. Katheryn's favorite was butter pecan and of course they didn't have it, so she decided on vanilla with caramel.

As she left the shop, she brought the ice cream cone up to her mouth for her first anticipated bite, and at the same time this man ran into her; her ice cream went all over her face, up her nose, and down the front of her blouse. She was furious, and the young man, although apologetic, was laughing so hard he could not talk. Katheryn tried to clean the ice cream with the one small napkin, but it wasn't working. The young man noticed and ran into the ice cream shop to get more napkins. When he returned he found Katheryn with tears rolling down her cheeks mingling with the ice cream. Jonathan O'Conner felt as he had been hit in the gut, he was now so sorry and anything he tried to do to help didn't. He apologized profusely, but it didn't seem to help either. He watched her throw napkins soiled with ice cream into a bin and walk away. As Jonathan stood there watching Katheryn leaving, he felt so sorry for her, knowing he had something to do with spoiling her day. He had not ever seen her before, but he did notice, even covered with ice cream, she was beautiful.

When Katheryn got back to her apartment she just sat and had a good cry, took a shower, put on her pajamas, and picked up a brochure about Scotland. She hoped she never saw that stupid guy again. He should watch where he is going, and he was a horrible person for ruining her ice cream she wanted so badly. Katheryn said quietly, "Happy Fourth of July, Katheryn," as she drifted off to sleep.

Chapter 13

As Katheryn walked through the halls of Oxford she couldn't help to feel a sense of pride knowing she had been accepted at this wonderful, old establishment of learning. To be able to work on her master's at Oxford was a dream of Grand's but soon became hers. She was thankful and felt blessed as she explored to find her first lecturing hall. It was quite impressive, and she took mental notes to tell Grand the next time they spoke. As she found a seat she looked around and noticed the hall was filling up. Katheryn thought, *This looks to be a full class.* She sat down in a seat about middle way and in the center.

She thought this would be excellent, and she would have a straight view of the professor. Katheryn gathered herself and took out her notebook and pens. She was ready. As the professor walked in the hall, the room became quiet. The professor wrote his name on the board with chalk, Jonathan O'Conner, then he turned around and spoke. Katheryn just closed her eyes and said to herself, "Wonderful, just wonderful. This could not be." Is this the same guy that slammed into her on the Fourth of July causing her to almost inhale her ice cream cone? As Jonathan O'Conner spoke Katheryn heard nothing; evidently he said he would be leading the class today for Professor Hayden and that Professor Hayden would be here for his next lecture.

Jonathan O'Conner was working on his doctorate in history. Katheryn heard that. She watched him as he spoke to the class; she had to admit he was good. She saw nothing of the idiot that ran into her and stood there laughing at her hysterically. Jonathan O'Conner showed a presence, and you could clearly see he owned his class. He was definitely in command, and Katheryn hated to admit again, he was a good and a great speaker. When the class was over she tried to slip out and not make eye contact with him. When she got through the door she thought, *I've made it.* Katheryn walked fast to escape, and as she turned a corner, guess who she runs smack into—Jonathan O'Conner. Katheryn thought, *How did he get here?* He looked straight into her eyes and said, "Hello." Katheryn said hello, and that was it! He continued quickly on his way, and Katheryn thought, *He didn't recognize me!* With a sigh of relief, she shook her head and walked out into a wet misty day thinking, *I am going to have to purchase an umbrella.* As she walked with her head down, while everyone else walked under an umbrella, Katheryn thought, *Everyone is probably saying, "Dumb American."* "Well, it doesn't rain every day in Abbeville, South Carolina!" Katheryn said out loud.

Katheryn's life started involving into a routine. She had explored the beautiful historical campus on days she didn't have a class, and now she was in the Bodleian Library, the main research library at Oxford. It was the second largest Library in the UK only after the British Library. She loved spending time here, and now she was researching for information on the two British soldiers that overtook her ancestors' village and farms; she knew in her heart, the information she needed would be found here. As Katheryn was looking through documents in the 1775 era for troops and names sent to the American colonies, she hit a dead end. She decided to call it a day; she had been at this for six hours. Before she left, as she was signing out, she looked up and saw Jonathan O'Conner talking to a very attractive girl. They were in her path to leave, so she waited. In a few minutes they both walked over to another isle, so she left, thinking, *How in the world does one keep running into the same person on this campus unintentionally? Good grief!*

When Katheryn arrived at her apartment she was soaked to the bone. She took a hot shower to warm up, got into her pajamas, and decided to call Grand. She dialed and waited to be connected. Soon she heard Grand's sweet voice say, "Hello."

Katheryn immediately said, "Hello, Great-grandmother, it is Katheryn."

After the phone call ended Katheryn reflected on their conversation, which was so different from her parents. Grand was interested in her as a person, wanting to know about her feelings and her life, not her accomplishments. Although Grand was very proud of what she had done, she was also very loving. Katheryn thought, *I am so blessed God gave me Grand. She is all I need.*

Thanksgiving was approaching and Grand had offered to buy her a ticket to come home, but Katheryn declined. She wasn't on the same schedule as at home, but she would definitely go home for Christmas. Katheryn missed her family and mostly her great-grandmother, whom she fondly referred to as "Grand." She knew Grand was getting up in years, but she was the loveliest Southern lady, full of charm and grace she had ever known. Katheryn also knew Grand had been and still was her number one cheerleader. Katheryn cared for her parents, but they just expected what she did or accomplished the norm—no fanfare from them and no love. And that was how she grew up. She did what was expected, and that was it. No "good job, kid." No "I am so proud of you." These were what she got from Grand and not her parents. Katheryn really spent more time living with her great-grandmother than her parents, and this is where her love came from, her Grand.

Every time she talked to Grand, there was always the famous question: have you met any handsome young men yet? Katheryn would always answer with her same reply: "No, Grand, but you will be the first to know." Grand would always come back with "You will soon, my dear."

Chapter 14

Thanksgiving came and went. The closest thing Katheryn could find to celebrate was a chicken sandwich, which she called pitiful.

A few days before Katheryn was to leave for home to spend Christmas she discovered a lead on one of the two names she had found before during her research in college. There were two British officers in charge of the area where her ancestors' farms were located in Virginia, in or around the time of the Revolutionary War. Katheryn's ancestors left the area sometime around 1775 and migrated to Abbeville, South Carolina, due to the British soldiers confiscating their farms. Katheryn had these facts, but this is where her research had gone cold during college. Today, three days before she was supposed to leave for home for Christmas holidays, she found information on one of the officers. His name was Alexander Delgrave. Everything matched up; everything she found was leading to this Alexander Delgrave. She also found out where he was from—a place called Newton Abbot in Devon, approximately 168 miles from Oxford. Katheryn was thrilled. She was already trying to see if she could take a train to Newton Abbot before she had to leave for home. If she could only squeeze one day in to check grave sites and the local parish before she left, it would be tight but she thought she could do it. Katheryn thought, *I am an American. We drive 168 miles at a drop of a hat with no problem!*

The next morning Katheryn packed her backpack with what she needed for overnight and went to the train station. She bought her ticket and sat down to wait for her train that would be arriving soon. She figured it would take approximately three hours to get there, but then she added the time for the changing trains, so she should be there in four hours and fifteen minutes. Katheryn boarded her train, found her window seat, and settled in. She glanced out the window, she saw a group of young people walking past, and she could have sworn she saw Jonathan O'Conner. She thought, *Really?* Katheryn passed it off as a lookalike and the fact she was constantly paranoid about running into him. Katheryn's view was, *I haven't seen him since the time I saw him in the library, so maybe that curse is broken.* The train was beginning to move, and she was feeling the excitement starting to build and hoping she would have some news to take back home for Grand.

Katheryn pulled a book out of her backpack that held history about Newton Abbot. As she read she found out that Newton Abbot was on the River Teign in the Teignbridge District of Devon and had been a market town for over seven hundred years. She studied her map and found the town of Newton Abbot was south of Oxford and close to the English Channel to get a better understanding of her location. Katheryn was engrossed in her book when all of a sudden a loud group of people came through on their way to the dining car or bar; she was sure it was the bar. Katheryn was a little jealous as she watched them pass by. You could see they were all friends and totally enjoyed each other's company. As Katheryn watched the group pass by, she thought, *I miss that.* So far she had not made any friends at Oxford other than Oliver, and she rarely saw him, really only in passing. She mentally counted and calculated there must be about ten of them. As they moved quickly through the car there was one straggler; a few of the group yelled back, "Come on, Jonathan! Keep up, mate." Katheryn felt herself stiffen, thinking, *No, it couldn't be!* As the group of friends headed for the dining car, Jonathan finally made his way past her, and she could clearly see it was one and the same—her ice cream attacker, Jonathan. She could not believe he was on the same train. Katheryn's mind was really asking the questions now, and the number one question was, why? *Why do I keep running into the same guy, and he doesn't even recognize me! He doesn't even know that I am the one he ran into on Fourth of July.*

Then she had a small sadness come over her as she watched Jonathan close the door to the car. *He has friends, and I don't.* Also, that glass of wine she thought about having later was not happening now. As Katheryn glanced at her watch she figured the train would be stopping soon, and she would be changing trains. That would surely take care of Jonathan O'Conner's group, she silently hoped.

All of a sudden the conductor came over the intercom and said they would be arriving in Bristol in fifteen minutes. Katheryn pulled her long blond hair up into a ponytail then put her ball cap on and guided her ponytail through the opening in the back of her cap. She started to put her sunglasses on, but she suddenly thought, *Why in the world did I bring these? The sun never shines in England!* She crammed everything back into her backpack, put her coat back on, and waited for the train to stop with her new umbrella in her hand. She knew everyone that saw her would probably think or know she was an American, because she didn't think she had ever seen a girl so far in England with a ball cap on. Katheryn said quietly to herself, "I am proud to be an American, and I love my favorite old cap from college. It has been with me through many of a bad hair day!"

The train came to a stop, and several people started getting up to disembark. Katheryn stepped off the train into a mist, she hurried through the train station to see where to go to catch her next train to Newton Abbot. She walked up to the arrival and departure boards and found her train and platform. As she turned to go, a young man walked straight into her causing her to drop her umbrella. As she reached down to pick it up, so did he, bumping her head with his satchel to the point of knocking her off balance. Katheryn literally sat down on the floor. She looked at the young man and said, "Really?" He tried to help her up, but she just held her hand up to let him know she did not need him and got up on her own. Katheryn brushed herself off. The young man was still apologizing as Katheryn started to walk off. The young man said, "Please wait." Katheryn turned and recognized him immediately; it was Jonathan O'Conner. Jonathan pleaded, "Please let me buy you a cup of tea. Please, I am so sorry."

Katheryn replied, "That will not be necessary."

Jonathan looked at the girl and knew there was something familiar about her, but he couldn't put a finger on it. "You are American," Jonathan stated.

Katheryn looked at him and said, "Yes, I am," then turned and walked away.

Jonathan was still standing there watching her when the lightbulb came on; she was the ice cream girl. He went after her, but she was gone just like before. Jonathan thought, *This girl must hate me. I keep causing her pain.*

Katheryn found her train. They were already allowing people to board, so she hurried and found her car, hopped on, and found her seat. She sat down, took a deep breath, and thoughts whirling in her mind were *What is up with this guy? Every time I turn around, there he is trying to cause harm to my body! What is this?* Katheryn could not get a grip on why this was happening, and what drove her crazy was, he never recognized her! She finally settled down and laid back, looking out the window at the people passing, wondering who they were and where they were going. Did they have families? Were they happy? Did they have somewhere to go for Christmas? The train gave a small jolt and started moving.

Katheryn's journey had certainly started off with a peculiar event, and she was hoping the rest of her journey would be normal. She wanted to get to her destination, do some research and hopefully find some new information on Alexander Delgrave, then head home for Christmas.

Katheryn arrived in Newton Abbot later than she had calculated, so she took a cab to her hotel, the Union Inn. Usually she would have walked to see the town, but it was pouring down rain, of course, and cold—bitter cold. The Union Inn was charming and had a wonderful roaring fire in the dining area and in the sitting area also where the bar was located. Katheryn checked in and went up to her room. The room was very nice with a high poster bed and a small sitting area. She looked out the window and wondered where Jonathan O'Conner ended up today. She only gave that thought process a moment after she heard her stomach growl. She was famished, and the aroma from the dining room downstairs was calling her. Katheryn went downstairs to the dining room. It was sit-where-you-want, so she grabbed a small table near the fireplace. She looked around and soaked up the quaintness of the inn. She thought, *One day, I would love to come back here. The waiter was great, and the meal was so, so good!* Katheryn looked out the window, and it was still pouring down rain, so she decided she would stay in and hit some grave sites in the morning.

The next morning she was up and downstairs for breakfast, which consisted of tea and a croissant, and out the door. The weather was misty and cold. Last evening she mapped out her route, and everything was within walking distance. She had to be at the station at three, so she didn't have a lot of time. She would have to hurry. The first graveyard proved no results, neither did the second, but the third she found something. There were several graves with the name Delgrave on them. Katheryn took out her camera and snapped pictures of every Delgrave she saw.

She looked at her watch. It said two o'clock. She reluctantly left and headed for the train station.

She arrived with twenty minutes to spare. Katheryn thought, *I am cutting it short!* She found her train, found her car, got on, and found her seat. As she settled down she went over her notes. She heard a noise and looked out the window to see where it came from, but all she could see was it had started to snow. Katheryn smiled and thought, *How lovely! The town of Newton Abbot and the residents will have a white Christmas.* The train started to move, and Katheryn relaxed and watched the snow out her window as she drifted off to sleep. The next thing Katheryn heard were screams and the loud twisting of metal, then everything went black.

Chapter 15

The Newton Abbot hospital was on high alert; all doctors were called in, and patients were coming in so fast from the train wreck they didn't have anywhere to put them. One of the doctors did a quick examination on a young lady with a broken leg and a possible concussion. The young lady also had a nasty gash on her left arm. The doctor sent her to X-ray and surgery. The night was absolutely a nightmare for all concerned. One of the nurses said out loud, *"Thank God we haven't lost one yet."*

The staff worked all though the night and the next day. Finally, everyone was placed where they could get the right care for their injuries. Dr. O'Conner checked on the last of his patients before he left for home; the young lady with the broken leg was in a coma. He looked at her chart then he looked down at his patient and felt sadness because she was alone. The authorities were desperately trying to match names and patients. They hadn't found out who the young lady was yet. She lay there so still as Dr. O'Conner examined her. Dr. O'Conner said to the young lady, "I will be back in the morning unless there is an emergency, and hopefully we will find out who you are." He left for home, exhausted.

The next morning in the O'Conner house, there was a flurry of activity with a lot of questions. Jonathan listened to his dad tell about the train wreck and all the patients. His father continued to talk about this young woman with a broken leg and in a coma. He also said they did not know who she was as of last night. Jonathan thought, *Poor girl,* as he grabbed a muffin to make sure he got one with three sisters in the house.

Dr. O'Conner left for the hospital, and Jonathan tried to find a quiet place to study, but that didn't seem to be happening anytime soon. He heard his mother calling for him to run an errand for her. She needed him to go to the hospital to take something important to his father. Jonathan answered, "Yes, my lovely mother, is there anything else you desire?"

She looked at him and laughed. She gave him a kiss on the cheek and said, "Thank you, my one and only son."

Jonathan smiled and said, "Whatever you need, Mrs. O'Conner." He grabbed the package for his father and his mother's keys. The hospital was not far away, but he thought he might do a little Christmas shopping while he was out, so he would take his mum's car. He reached the hospital and pulled into the car park. He grabbed the package for his father and walked down the stairs in the car park, crossed the lawn, and into the hospital. His father would be making his rounds, so he went to the nurses' station. The nurse said he was in room 501. Jonathan walked down the hall to room 501 and peeked in. His father saw him, held up one finger to him, and said, "Just a minute." Dr. O'Conner was finishing up with the patient's chart. He looked down at the young lady with compassion and said, "I will be back in a little while." The young lady was still in a coma, but Dr. O'Conner hoped she would hear him and come out of it soon. Dr. O'Conner walked out into the hall where he met his son. Jonathan handed his father the package, and Dr. O'Conner said, "Oh, thank you, son."

Jonathan smiled at his dad and asked, "Is that the young girl? Have they found out who she is?"

Dr. O'Conner answered his son, "Yes, she is the one, and no, they haven't found out who she is yet." Dr. O'Conner looked at his son and asked, "Jonathan, would you read to her?"

Jonathan looked at his father with a questionable look and answered, "Yes, I will, good way for me to study."

Dr. O'Conner patted his son on the shoulder and said, "Good man."

Jonathan went to the car and grabbed his satchel. He went back into the hospital to room 501. He entered the room and looked at the young girl lying in the bed. There was something instantly familiar; he took a closer look and said, "It is you!

The American, it is you!" Jonathan looked down at this beautiful creature and thought, *You are the ice cream girl.* Jonathan ran from the room to find his father. He saw him down the hall at the nurses' station. He walked fast and took his father's arm. "I know this girl. I have seen her several times. She is an American."

Dr. O'Conner looked at his son and asked, "Are you sure? A hundred percent sure?"

Jonathan answered his father with "Yes, one hundred percent."

Dr. O'Conner immediately made a phone call to the authorities. After he hung up the phone, he looked at Jonathan and said, "They informed me that they would send someone over to the hospital right away."

Jonathan went back to room 501 and pulled a chair up to the bed and started reading to Katheryn.

A couple of hours later the authorities came into the room and asked Jonathan to step outside in the hall. The officers came out into the hall where Jonathan was waiting and asked Jonathan questions, but all he could say was she was an American and he believed she might go to Oxford but he wasn't sure. The officers walked back into Katheryn's room and confirmed who she was by her passport picture. They had found her backpack, and it held all her information. The officers explained their findings with Dr. O'Conner, who she was and where she was from. She was a grad student at Oxford, and they told Dr. O'Conner they would contact her family. Jonathan was not privy to the information the officers told his father. After the officers left, Jonathan pleaded with his father to please give him some information on Katheryn. Dr. O'Conner thought it would be good for Jonathan to know some information since he was willing to read to her, so he told his son she is a student at Oxford, she is an American, and her name is Katheryn Wardlaw Kensington.

Jonathan went back into Katheryn's room, sat beside her bed, and said, "Katheryn, I am here. My name is Jonathan, and I will stay with you." Jonathan stayed the night with her; he just couldn't leave her alone. Before he read to her each time, he would say, "Katheryn Wardlaw Kensington, I am going to read to you now." Dr. O'Conner talked to Katheryn's father. He wanted to bring her back to the States, but Dr. O'Conner said it would be too dangerous to move her right now, so they would keep in touch on her progress.

Emilia Wardlaw Kensington, Katheryn's great-grandmother, was devastated. She was so upset, and she decided she would come to her great-granddaughter's side. Emilia could not understand what was wrong with her parents, but she knew they had always been that way. *Why did they not get on a plane immediately?* "Well," Emilia said, "I will!"

Chapter 16

On December 23, Jonathan O'Conner sat beside Katheryn Wardlaw Kensington's bed. The light from the morning sun was starting to filter in causing a glow in Katheryn's room. Jonathan sat and looked at the beautiful girl lying lifeless in her hospital bed. It had been two weeks, and there had not been any change in Katheryn's condition. As Jonathan watched her he wondered if she could hear anything he said. He had read to her every day since the accident. Some nights he would just stay with her because she seemed so alone and fragile. The nurse came into the room to take care of Katheryn's needs;

Jonathan knew the drill by now. He would go to the cafe and get a cup of tea.

He ran into his father, Dr. O'Conner. Jonathan asked his father if he thought Katheryn would ever come out of the coma. Dr. O'Conner said, "Comas are tricky, son, but I fully believe she will. It just takes time for things to heal." Dr. O'Conner looked at his son. *He was a wonderful son,* he thought, *bright and heading for his professorship.* Dr. O'Conner could not be prouder of his son. Not only was he an excellent scholar, but he had compassion. Dr. O'Conner smiled, put his arm around Jonathan, and said, "I could not be prouder of you, son. You would have been a great doctor!" Then he added, "As well as a history professor." Jonathan smiled at his father. He knew his father had wanted him to follow in his footsteps, but he never pushed him to. Jonathan's father had been completely supportive on the path he chose.

They walked back together to room 501. When they reached Katheryn's room they found a beautiful older lady sitting by her bed holding her hand and talking sweetly to her. "You are going to be fine, my dear. We will have all those adventures we talked about. You will go back to Oxford." Emilia Wardlaw Kensington looked up to see the two gentlemen standing at the door. Dr. O'Conner walked in with Jonathan and introduced himself and Jonathan. Emilia said, with all her American Southern grace, "Hello, I am Emilia Wardlaw Kensington, Katheryn's great-grandmother. Are you her doctor?"

Dr. O'Conner replied, "Yes." The questions started, and Dr. O'Conner explained everything with complete patience. Emilia thanked him for everything they had done and thanked Jonathan for reading to her precious great-granddaughter. Emilia explained she would go back to the hotel to rest and would be back later. Dr. O'Conner assured Mrs. Kensington that Katheryn was being well taken care of and if there was any change she would be called. After Emilia left, Dr. O'Conner said to his son, "What a wonderful and graceful lady. That is what they refer to when they say, she was a breath of fresh air." Jonathan agreed with his father with a smile.

Emilia had checked into a hotel near the hospital. She thought her suite at the hotel would be sufficient and she hired a car and driver, so she was set. Her traveling companion would be handling anything else they needed. Rose had been with Emilia for years. She not only worked for Emilia; she was a valued friend. Emilia told Rose after they rested from their trip they would take turns sitting with Katheryn. Emilia looked out the window with a heavy heart and prayed, "My dear Lord, be with our girl."

Jonathan stayed with Katheryn after her great-grandmother left. He held her hand and talked to her about Oxford, her great-grandmother, her beauty, and the first time they met. When he said the word *ice cream,* her index finger moved on the hand he was holding. As Jonathan talked softly to Katheryn he watched her hand in hopes of another movement, but it didn't happen. Jonathan also prayed, and after he finished he looked at Katheryn and said, "Let's just talk a while, Katheryn. I really like your great-grandmother. She is the epitome of grace, charm, and very Southern like you. I remember the day I ran into you, Katheryn, and as you walked away, I felt so bad for spoiling your day, much less your ice cream. If it helps in any small way, even the smallest, I thought you were absolutely beautiful, even covered in ice cream! Please forgive me, Katheryn, and wake up. I want to talk to you and hear your lovely voice. Please fight to come back, Katheryn. We are all here waiting for you." Jonathan picked up her hand and kissed it, then held it in his.

Standing in the doorway listening was Emilia Wardlaw Kensington. She thought, *Why haven't you told me about this extraordinary young gentleman, my dear child?* Emilia walked over to Jonathan, laid her frail hand on his shoulder, and said, "You need a break, sir. Go home and rest. We will sit with her this evening." Jonathan looked up and smiled. He immediately stood up and said he didn't mind staying, but Emilia insisted he get some fresh air and rest. Emilia said to Jonathan, "Young man, I know how long you have been here and what you have done for my Katheryn. I am indebted. Now please do as I say, and I will see you tomorrow on Christmas Eve." Jonathan reluctantly left, and on the way home, he stopped at a shop to finish his

Christmas shopping. He wanted to buy a present also for Kathrine.

Emilia and Rose sat with Katheryn for the rest of the evening, and Emilia told Katheryn what a wonderful young man Jonathan was. "I think he might be your one, precious girl! Wake up, my dear, you have much to enjoy." Emilia and Rose got ready to leave and instructed the nurse to please call if there was a slightest change.

As Emilia and Rose got into the car, Rose looked at her friend and said with the utmost care, "Emilia, I have a good feeling about Katheryn. She will be fine."

Emilia patted Rose on her hand and said, "I think you are right, my dear friend."

Chapter 17

Christmas came and went with no change in Katheryn's condition. Jonathan, Rose, and Emilia had taken turns sitting with Katheryn for the last week. Jonathan said he wanted to be with her on New Year's Eve, and Emilia gave in. Emilia went back to their hotel for some rest, and she said she would see him tomorrow at his parents' home. Dr. O'Conner and his wife had thoughtfully invited Emilia and Rose to their home for New Year's Day dinner, and they graciously accepted.

Jonathan sat looking at Katheryn. Her room held flowers that had not been admired by her and presents she had not opened. Jonathan took her hand in his and said, "Katheryn, please wake up, please come back. We are waiting for you." There was no response. Jonathan picked up the newspaper and began to read, and then he heard in a low strained voice, "Can you not find something more interesting to read than the local news?"

Jonathan's mouth dropped. He collected himself and asked, "Katheryn, can you hear me?"

Katheryn's voice was low and raspy, but she said, "Yes."

Jonathan sprang up and ran down the hall to the nurses' station, blurting out, "She's awake, she's awake!"

The nurses ran to room 501. Jonathan called his father. Everyone was elated; she was awake. In no time the hall outside Katheryn's room was full of people cheering her on. Jonathan patiently waited until he could see her. Dr. O'Conner came out of her room and looked at his anxious son with concern. Dr. O'Conner put his arm around Jonathan and guided him to an area down the hall for privacy and said, "I am pretty sure she is on her way to a full recovery, son." Jonathan was thankful and relieved. Dr. O'Conner and Jonathan walked back to room 501 to wait outside in the hall.

Katheryn's great-grandmother Emilia Wardlaw Kensington asked for Jonathan to come into the room. He walked in the room nervously and thought, *What is wrong with me? I stand in front large groups of people to lecture all the time.* He walked up to Mrs. Kensington. She took his hand and turned to her great-granddaughter and said, "This is the young gentleman I told you about. He has been at your side for days." She leaned down and kissed Katheryn on the forehead and said, "I will give you two a little time."

Jonathan sat down in the chair beside her bed. Katheryn thought, *Why do I keep running into this guy?* Jonathan spoke first. "I am so happy for you, Katheryn. By the way, my name is Jonathan O'Conner."

Katheryn thought, *Why is he so handsome?* then she said, "I know your name."

He asked, "How?"

Katheryn answered, "You taught my first class at Oxford. It was after you ran into me. You owe me a double-scoop vanilla cone with caramel!"

Jonathan started laughing, and so did Katheryn. Jonathan said kindly, "I promise you ten double-cone vanilla caramel ice creams, whenever you want them!"

Katheryn answered, "I will definitely take you up on it!"

The clock struck twelve, and Jonathan looked at Katheryn with caring eyes and said, "Happy New Year, Katheryn Wardlaw Kensington." He got up and kissed her on her forehead; it was the same thing he did every time he left her.

Katheryn said to Jonathan, "Happy New Year, Professor Jonathan O'Conner." Jonathan stayed for a while until she drifted off to sleep, then he left for home.

The next morning at the hospital, they were getting Katheryn up for exercise, and when Jonathan got to her room he had to stop himself. He was used to just walking into her room. He tapped on the door, and he heard Katheryn say, "Come in." She was sitting in a chair looking lovely as ever.

Jonathan said, "Good morning, Katheryn."

She said, "Good morning, Professor O'Conner."

Jonathan smiled and asked Katheryn, "How are you on this fine, cold, and rainy morning, Miss Katheryn?"

She answered, "Fine, a little weak, leg aches, and physical therapy is really hard, but other than that I am great. How are you?"

Jonathan sat down on Katheryn's bed, smiled at her, and answered her, saying, "I am great now, since you are better."

Dr. O'Conner walked in with Emilia. Jonathan asked if he should step outside, and everyone said, "No, stay." Dr. O'Conner told Katheryn she was doing good, blood work was excellent, and all other tests looked great. Dr. O'Conner continued to say, "All we need for you to do now is heal that leg and take it easy for a few weeks, and of course you need to do physical therapy and a plan to go home."

Katheryn said, "Really? Wonderful! I need to get back to Oxford, my classes and—"

Dr. O'Conner cut her off and said, "Wait a minute, you are getting ahead of yourself." He told her she could go home provided she had some help and for the next three weeks she would have to take it easy. Then Dr. O'Conner explained she would see a very good friend of his, Dr. Sommers, at Oxford. "Your leg will have to be monitored, Ms. Kensington."

Katheryn said, "Yes, sir."

Jonathan said he could help and was met with no, would be too much trouble, can hire someone, etc. Jonathan said, "I can help her with assignments. I can take her food. She will be fine, I promise."

After a couple more rounds of maybe and maybe not, it was settled. Jonathan would help her, and if it was too much to handle, Mrs. Kensington would hire someone to come in and help. Mrs. Kensington announced she would hire a car and driver to deliver them back to Oxford and be on duty for anything Katheryn might need for the next three weeks or until the cast came off and she was a hundred percent healed. Everyone agreed, and it was settled.

Grand and Rose would go home, and Katheryn and Jonathan would go back to Oxford in a few days.

Katheryn cried when Grand left; she knew Grand loved her much more than her own parents, if they loved her at all. Jonathan found her sobbing when he came into her room. He went into alarm mode. "What's wrong? You want me to get the nurse?"

Katheryn looked at him with tears running down her cheeks and said, "Grand just left."

Jonathan was relieved but felt so sorry for her; she had been through so much. He sat down on the side of her bed, reached out and pulled her into his arms, and held her while she cried. She kept saying, "I don't know what is wrong with me. This isn't me. I am usually pretty strong, had to be with the parents I grew up with." Jonathan just let her get it all out. She had a good cry, and it was probably the best thing she could do at the moment. Jonathan just patted her and kept saying everything will get better. He had calmed down his sisters before, so he had plenty of practice.

After a good while she looked up at him and said, "Thank you, thank you so much, Jonathan."

Jonathan told her, "You are welcome. You know I have to make it up to you for the ice cream incident, not to mention the incident in the train station. Heck, I need all the points I can get."

Katheryn smiled, and he kissed her on top of her head. Jonathan stood up and looked straight into her eyes and asked, "You okay?"

She answered, "Yes, much better. Thank you." Jonathan brought a book of poems with him from his parents' library; he showed it to Katheryn for approval. She said, "Oh yes!"

Jonathan began to read to Katheryn. As he turned the page, he looked at her and smiled, thinking, *She is still fragile,* but he was confident she would heal quick in the days to come, and he would be there to help in any way he could.

Chapter 18

On the ride back to Oxford, Katheryn explained to Jonathan why she was in Newton Abbot, about her research, and her family's history. She asked him if she was boring him and to please tell her. He said no. Jonathan said he loved history and especially history with a twist of mystery in it. She picked up her backpack, which was pretty much intact after the train wreck, but she was afraid her camera might be damaged. She told Jonathan, "I took pictures of the grave sites with the name Delgrave, but if the camera is damaged I can always go back to take more pictures."

Jonathan, with a serious face, said, "Delgrave... that name is familiar."

Katheryn told Jonathan there were many Delgraves buried at a cemetery in Newton Abbot. Katheryn laid back and closed her eyes; for some reason she became so sleepy. Jonathan thought about all she had said, and he loved her determination, even if it was like looking for a needle in a haystack. As Katheryn rested her eyes, she wondered if she should tell Jonathan that when she was in a coma she could hear everything he said, and she did fight to come back because of him.

They reached Oxford. Jonathan helped get Katheryn settled in her apartment and was glad she had a lift. He dropped by his apartment, checked on a couple of things, and left to get some groceries for Katheryn at the market. Jonathan was enjoying the fact he had a chauffeur; it made everything much easier.

He returned to Katheryn's with two bags full of groceries, hoping she liked what he had purchased. Katheryn tried to give him money, but he wouldn't take it. Jonathan prepared something for them to eat. After they ate, Jonathan cleaned up, then wrote down his number, explained to Katheryn to call for anything, and told her he meant it. She said, "Yes, I promise."

After Jonathan left she got into her bed and turn off the light and went to sleep. Around three in the morning, Katheryn woke up screaming. She was terrified with a coldness she couldn't shake and wondered why. She fell back to sleep after an hour or so with no more incidents.

The next morning she got up and wondered why she would be so scared. Then instantly, she knew what it was. It was the train wreck. She also knew this was something she would have to come to terms with and get through it.

The phone rang, and it was Jonathan checking in to see how she was. She let him know she was fine. He said he would check in later. She told him, "Thank you," and hung up the phone. Katheryn managed to make a bowl of cereal and started look-ing at her research. She called her driver and asked him to take the film of the graves to be developed. She was hoping she would get some pictures. The driver was a really nice guy, very sweet, and probably old enough to be her father. He was glad to help in any way, and Katheryn was sure Grand was taking care of him.

Katheryn's classes didn't start for another two weeks, so she would use this time to continue her research on the Delgraves.

Jonathan was real busy; this was his last semester, and after years of working for his goal, it was finally in sight. He wanted to be a professor of history for as long as he could remember, and now his dream was coming true. Katheryn would go through his mind like a wave. He wondered if she was okay. He wondered if she needed anything. Then he would stop and call her. The last time he called, Katheryn said, "Jonathan, I am fine. Please do what you need to do. Seriously, I am okay." Jonathan thought, *I am being ridiculous. I need to give her space. She will let me know if she needs anything.* He rushed to get to a lecture he was giving, while trying not to think about Katheryn, but it didn't last. Something about her would creep into his thoughts, and he would smile.

Katheryn learned the driver's name when he returned with her pictures. His name was Charles, Charles Finley. She thanked Charles and sent him on his way. Katheryn opened the envelope that held the pictures. She was so excited; they all were perfect. She laid them all out on the table. She found her magnifying glass and went to work. Katheryn cross-referenced and believed she might, just maybe, have an ancestral line worked out. She could now trace Alexander Delgrave to his grandson, Emerson Delgrave. She now had three generations. Katheryn thought, *This is a good start.* She pushed back from the table, tired and stiff from sitting at the table all day. She forgot to eat lunch, so now she was really hungry. She got up and hobbled to the kitchen, and the phone rang. She grabbed it and, leaning against the wall, answered, "Hello."

Jonathan said, "Hey there, how are you?"

Katheryn said, "Doing good."

Jonathan asked her if she had eaten, and she said no. He said, "Good, I will be there in a few minutes with Chinese, do you like?"

Katheryn said, "Yes, thank you! See you soon." Katheryn was thankful. Now she would not have to fix something to eat, and she was thankful for Jonathan; he really had been a prince of a guy.

Jonathan arrived with food in tow. Katheryn was famished, and the food smell so good. They ate and caught up. Jonathan was surprised she had discovered three generations. Katheryn was also excited that she would finally get her cast off the next day and go to a soft cast. Jonathan offered to go with her, but she said she would be fine and she had her man Charles. Jonathan said, "Charles is a good guy."

Katheryn agreed. Jonathan needed to go and helped get everything cleaned up. Katheryn thanked him, and he was gone. Katheryn wondered what he had to do. *Maybe study,* she thought. She got ready for bed and was looking forward to tomorrow, to hopefully get her heavy cast off.

The next day Charles picked Katheryn up for her doctor's appointment. After an X-ray the doctor gave Katheryn good news: the cast was coming off today. The soft cast was so much better to manage, and she could take it off to get into the shower.

Things were looking up. As they were leaving the doctor's office, Katheryn asked Charles if he would just take her for a short ride anywhere. Charles answered, "Your wish is my command, madam."

Katheryn said, "Thank you, Charles."

They rode through and around Oxford and out for a few miles to the suburbs. Katheryn thought the area was really pretty with manicured lawns even in the winter. As they were coming back, they passed a cute little pub not too far from the university called The Wooden Nickel. The car stopped for traffic. As Katheryn looked over at the pub, she saw Jonathan and the girl from the library walk in together. She thought as the car started to move, *He was just being nice to me, nothing else.* Seeing them made Katheryn's heart hurt just a little, but now she knew what he really thought. He was just being a friend. Jonathan was a nice guy, but evidently he was taken. This saddened Katheryn.

Chapter 19

Emilia Wardlaw Kensington summoned Katheryn's parents for tea at exactly three o'clock on a Thursday afternoon. She was thankful Katheryn was okay and doing well now. Her cast had come off, and it wouldn't be long before she could shed her soft one. It was the first of February, and she braced herself because she had a lot to say to these two people today coming for tea.

Katheryn's parents, Emerson and Nancy Kensington, arrived at exactly five minutes to three. Rose brought them into the sitting room to meet with Emilia. Emerson said, "Hello, Grandmother. It has been a while since we have had tea together."

Emilia sharply said, "Sit down, Emerson. We have some things to discuss."

After Rose served the tea, Emilia started to speak and ask both Emerson and Nancy to please not interrupt her until she was finished.

"As you know, I went to England to visit your daughter, Katheryn, do you remember her? She lay in a coma for three weeks with a concussion and broken leg, which she received from a train wreck. Did you ever call her? Did you ever go to see her? She could have died! Emerson, your parents would roll over in their graves if they knew how you have acted toward that precious girl! Not to say your sister, why she would give you Katheryn is totally beyond me. When my precious son and his wife, which were your parents Emerson, along with your sister and her husband died in that car crash, you were supposed to raise Katheryn as your own, but you never did!" Emerson tried to say something, and Emilia shut him down. Emilia continued, "Now listen to me, Emerson. This is what is going to happen!

Katheryn is approaching the age she will receive her trust left to her by my son and her parents. You cannot have it; it does not belong to you! Thank God, my son and your sister left this part of this debacle to me. Katheryn needs to be told the truth, and I will tell her immediately; it is way overdue."

Emerson got up and said, "Do what you want." He looked at his wife and said, "Nancy, we are leaving."

They left and Emilia could not believe that Emerson was her grandson. He was rude, arrogant, and a complete disappointment and totally out of her will.

As Emilia sat and finished her tea, she contemplated what she would say to her precious Katheryn and when. She knew this would have to be dealt with delicately. She did not want to upset her, but she had to know the truth. Many times Emilia wanted to tell her, but the way the trust was set up she couldn't, or Katheryn would lose her inheritance. Emilia knew she could not do this over the phone, she and Rose would travel to London and Katheryn could meet them there. She would ask that sweet, handsome Jonathan to come with her for support. The plan was set into motion, and Emilia hoped to be there by Valentine's Day.

Katheryn opened the letter from Grand. As she read she was elated to find out Grand and Rose were coming to London. She read on and found out Grand had taken care of her transportation to London and all she had to do is pack. Katheryn was so excited about the fact she had something to look forward to. The phone rang, and Katheryn picked it up and said, "Hello."

On the other end Jonathan said, "Hey, I have been trying to get in touch with you for two days. If you had not answered the phone, I was coming over."

Katheryn said, "I am fine, absolutely fine. You do not have to worry about me anymore. Really, I am good."

Jonathan quipped, "That wasn't the deal I made with your great-grandmother, and I think she would kill me if I did not do exactly as she ordered."

Katheryn laughed and said, "Don't worry, I will take care of Grand. Consider yourself off the hook as of now."

Jonathan asked, "Are you trying to get rid of me or something? Katheryn, I have one more job for dear Emilia. I am to accompany you to London in a few days, and I really like my neck, I wouldn't want Ms. Emilia to ring it!"

Katheryn breathed deeply and told Jonathan he did not have to come to London with her but he insisted, so she just gave in and said, "If this is what you want, then okay." Jonathan said he would see her in a few days unless she needed anything. Katheryn replied, "Okay, I will talk to you soon. Bye." She hung up the phone and sat down and said out loud, "I do not want him to come."

Jonathan said bye, but he didn't think Katheryn heard him. He could not understand why she had become so distant. He thought they got on well; he was really enjoying and looking forward to seeing her. He thought, evidently she did not feel the same. He was sorry. He thought things were different. He would get this London trip over with and leave her alone because that really seemed to be what she wanted.

Katheryn stared at the phone and said, "Why do you want to go to London with me when you have a girlfriend?" This she didn't get. And it was close to or on Valentine's. Do they do Valentine's in England? Katheryn shook her head and said, "I give up. I have no more to say on this subject."

Then she started thinking about what she would take to London and then stopped and said, "I am going to London. What a perfect time to do some major shopping!"

Chapter 20

Packed and ready to go, Katheryn waited patiently for Charles, her driver, to come and pick her up to go to London to see Grand. She was looking forward to this trip, and she had missed Grand and Rose so much. They were her family. Katheryn heard a knock at the door. She hobbled over and opened the door. She was expecting Charles, but she got Jonathan. He said, "Hey."

She answered, "Hey."

Jonathan got all her luggage, and she followed him to the elevator. He said for her to go down first and he would come second with the luggage.

Katheryn agreed and got on the elevator. When she got to the car Charles was standing there and said, "Good morning, Katheryn."

Katheryn said, "Good morning, Charles." Katheryn had insisted on them being on a first-name basis. He helped her in the car and laid her cane beside her. He knew she couldn't wait to be rid of the cane, and he had kept telling her it wouldn't be long. Jonathan walked up with her luggage, and Charles opened the trunk of the car and placed the luggage inside.

Jonathan got into the car, looked at Katheryn, and said, "London, here we come."

Katheryn smiled. For the next fifteen minutes, no one other than Charles spoke. Charles thought, *What is wrong with these two? I thought they liked each other.*

Katheryn finally spoke and asked Jonathan how he was doing and was he getting excited to be finishing his studies in a couple of months. Jonathan told Katheryn he was fine and he was really looking forward to teaching full-time. Jonathan looked at her profile and thought she was absolutely beautiful. She looked healed. Jonathan said, "Katheryn, you look amazing. To have gone through what you have, you look rested and healed."

Katheryn answered, "Thank you, Jonathan, and thank you for all your help. You have been wonderful."

Jonathan asked Katheryn how her research was going, and she told him, "Great." Katheryn explained how she had tracked three generations and believed she might have a fourth. He was happy for her and said if there was any way he could help, he would be glad to. Katheryn told him she might take him up on his offer. Charles said they would be at their destination in about twenty minutes. Katheryn looked at Jonathan and said, "I can't wait to see Grand and Rose." Jonathan smiled at Katheryn as he squeezed her hand. As Charles said they arrived in twenty minutes at the hotel. They got out and went in. Katheryn looked back at Charles and said, "Thank you, Charles."

He answered, "My privilege, madam."

Jonathan and Katheryn walked in the hotel and went to the hotel's front desk. Jonathan gave the desk clerk their names. The desk clerk handed two keys to Jonathan with a note. Jonathan read the note and told Katheryn that they were to meet Grand when they arrived. They went to their rooms to freshen up. In a few minutes Jonathan knocked on Katheryn's door. She opened the door, and Jonathan held his hand out and said, "Shall we, madam?"

Katheryn smiled and said, "Yes, we shall!" She laid her hand on his, and they were off to see Grand.

Emilia knew they would be there any minute. She was a tad bit nervous, but she knew this needed to be done and this was the time to do it. Emilia heard a knock at the door. Rose let them in. Everyone was so glad to see each other. For the first thirty minutes Emilia allowed everyone to catch up and have the tea served. Then she got down to business.

Katheryn looked around Grand's suite; it was the finest London had to offer short of the Buckingham Palace. Katheryn smiled and thought, *Of course Grand would stay nowhere but the Ritz Hotel in London! Well, she deserved it!* Emilia broke Katheryn's thought when she asked everyone to sit down. Everyone found a seat, and Jonathan made sure he was close to Katheryn as Grand requested.

Emilia started off with "Katheryn, you know I love you with all my heart, and as I proceed with what I am about to say, please remember that."

Katheryn looked puzzled and asked, "What is it, Grand? Are you okay?"

Emilia said, "Yes, my dear, I am fine, and it breaks my heart to have to tell you this—something I wanted to tell you long ago, but my hands were tied legally." Emilia dove in and explained to Katheryn the easiest way she thought she could. "Katheryn, my precious child, Emerson and Nancy are not your biological parents. They were your guardians after your parents and grandparents were tragically killed in a horrible car accident twenty-two years ago. I not only lost my son and his wife, I also lost my granddaughter and her husband. It was a terrible time for everyone, and your mother wanted her brother to be your guardian if anything ever happened to her. Why she would make that particular decision, I cannot understand. I wanted you so much, child, but he and that awful Nancy got you legally. I have been a constant source in your life since the day you were born. I hired the nanny that took care of you. I assure you, I would not have let anything hurt you. You actually stayed with me more than you ever stayed with them. You have a trust, a quite large trust, that you will soon receive. This trust would have been lost to you if I had told you all this before now. I was going to make sure Emerson did not get his greedy hands on it. As of your twenty-third birthday Emerson and Nancy have no hold on you. It is over. Katheryn, I know this is hard and a lot to take in, but you have to know if I could have changed this I would have. I love you, my dear, more than anything. Now I will answer any questions you may have."

Katheryn was stunned. Her entire life changed in a moment. She stood up and walked around the room with everyone watching her to see her reaction. Katheryn looked at Grand. She walked over to her and knelt down, laid her head on Grand's lap, and cried. Grand patted her and said, "I am so sorry, my darling, I am truly so sorry."

Katheryn looked up to Grand and said with tears, "It all makes sense to me now, Grand. They never loved me, never. All my love came from you and Rose. It has always been me and you, Grand, always. Grand, there is one thing I do not understand. Why is Jonathan O'Conner here? He has a girlfriend. It is Valentine's; he should be with her!"

With tears in his eyes, which is so unusual for the English, Jonathan got up and knelt beside Katheryn on the floor and said, "I do not have a girlfriend, Katheryn, unless you might want to step into that position." Then he got up gave her his hand and helped her up.

She declared, "I saw you with her, once in the library and then another time going into a restaurant."

Jonathan looked at her puzzled and thought, *Sally MacGregor?* "Tall, skinny girl with long brown hair?"

Katheryn said, "Yes."

Jonathan shook his head and exclaimed, "No, she is my assistant. She will take over my position when I receive my professorship!"

Katheryn, somewhat embarrassed, simply said, "Oh."

Emilia and Rose watched the two intently. Then, Katheryn turned to Grand and said, "To say the least, Grand, this is a lot to digest. I am a little bit overwhelmed, but I am glad Dad, I mean Emerson, is not my father and Nancy is not my mother."

Emilia stood up and put her arms around her girl and said, "I know, my love, this is over the top, but I assure you your parents were wonderful and they loved you very much. I know that for a fact. Your poor mother thought her brother was wonderful, but he isn't. My son was a precious man and loved you dearly, and so did your grandmother."

Katheryn sat down beside Jonathan, looked straight at him, smiled, then she said, "I might want to step into that position, Jonathan."

Jonathan picked her hand up and kissed it as his eyes remained on her. Emilia thought, *Yes, my dear, he might be the one.*

Chapter 21

Later that evening when Katheryn and Jonathan got back to her room, he opened her door, turned to her, took her into his arm, and kissed her. He pulled back, looked deep into her eyes, and then he kissed her again. Katheryn's arms went up around Jonathan's neck. It was the sweetest kiss she had ever experienced, and he knew at that very moment she was the love of his life. Jonathan said, "I know you have so much to think about, huge night of new information. Please rest and get some sleep. If you can't and need anything, I am right next door." He took both her hands in his and kissed both.

Katheryn smiled and said, "Thank you." He turned, and she went into room. Katheryn laid across her bed and said out loud, "Grand, you were right. You said I would know, and now I know. He is the one, and it is absolutely the most wonderful feeling in the world." She closed her eyes and drifted off to sleep fully clothed thinking about Jonathan's sweet kiss.

Over the next few days Katheryn adjusted to being an orphan, and it was okay; she never had any real closeness with Emerson and Nancy, so there was no real loss. Grand had always been her person, and besides, she had lived with her practically her entire life, had her own room at Grand's, and it was decorated just for her.

Katheryn was packing to leave, and it dawned on her that she had a trust. A trust—wow, she couldn't believe it! She was well-off for a girl of twenty-two, almost twenty-three. In March on her birthday she would receive her trust! Katheryn thought, *Well, that could help fund my research to find the ring!* With that thought, she laughed.

The goodbyes were painful. Katheryn missed Grand and Rose so much. Grand looked at Jonathan with a stern face and said, "You take care of my girl, Jonathan O'Conner, or you will answer to me personally!" Then she smiled and winked at him.

Jonathan replied, "Yes, ma'am, you have nothing to worry about, she is in good hands."

Grand said, "I am counting on that, Jonathan O'Conner."

Jonathan and Katheryn put the two ladies into their limo, and that was that. Grand and Rose were headed back to Abbeville, South Carolina, and Jonathan and Katheryn were headed back to Oxford with Charles. As Charles drove them back to the university, Katheryn looked over at Jonathan and said, "In March I am getting an apartment with a fireplace."

Jonathan just laughed and told her, "You are so practical, my sweet girl, but that sounds very nice." They laughed, held hands, and talked about everything. Charles noticed the change in them and smiled.

Everyone returned home safely—Emilia and Rose to Abbeville, South Carolina, and Katheryn and Jonathan to Oxford.

Time passed quickly and Katheryn was just about to lose her cane, and she was so happy. She did physical therapy every day to strengthen her leg. She worked out to also strengthen her entire body. She felt good and knew one day she wanted to hike in the highlands of Scotland. This was on her list of things to do. As Katheryn left the physical therapist's office, she looked over at an ice cream shop and thought of her and Jonathan's first encounter, remembering that she was a mess and he was hysterical.

Katheryn hopped into the car, and Charles said, "Where to now, madam?"

Katheryn said, "Let's go get a scoop of ice cream, Charles, at that cute little shop near the clock."

Charles said, "Absolutely." Charles drove to the clock tower where the ice cream shop was located, parked close, and asked Katheryn what she would like.

Katheryn said, "Double scoop vanilla with caramel."

Charles replied, "You got it." Charles went to take care of the ice creams, and Katheryn laid back in her seat to read, but first she looked out the window. She noticed there were so many people sitting out on the grass and on the benches. Benches were placed all over this area for students to sit, and it was also a great place to study. As Katheryn scanned what she called the clock park, she thought she saw Jonathan sitting on a blanket with a girl, the girl with brown hair she saw in the library and at the restaurant. She watched them, and it seemed innocent until brown-haired girl leaned over and kissed Jonathan and he fell back onto the blanket with his lips attached to hers. Charles walked up with the ice cream and startled Katheryn. Katheryn got out of the car, grabbed her two scoops of vanilla with caramel, and walked over to Jonathan and brown-haired girl. When Jonathan saw her, he pushed the brown-haired girl away and jumped to his feet. He yelled, "I can explain!"

Katheryn took the double-scoop vanilla ice cream with caramel and smashed it into Jonathan's face, neck, and chest. Then she turned around and started for the car with Jonathan following her. She got to the car, got in, and rolled her window down and said, "Hope you enjoyed your ice cream. Now you owe me two, but don't worry, now I do not like ice cream, so you are off the hook!" She closed the window and asked Charles to please take her home. Jonathan stood there with ice cream all over him watching the love of his life ride away. The brown-haired girl walked up and said, "Jonathan, I am so sorry."

Jonathan looked at her and said, "Stay away from me."

Katheryn's heart was broken. She went home, opened a bottle of wine, and said, "That is it. I mean it, I will never give my heart to another man!" The phone rang and Katheryn let the answering machine get it. It was Jonathan trying to explain that he didn't kiss her; she kissed him, and he was trying to get her off of him. He promised over and over he didn't. "Please, Katheryn, talk to me." The tape ran out on the answering machine, so he had to call back to finish his message. His messages were all the same, but the last time he called Katheryn heard something in his voice, it quivered. She almost felt sorry for him but shut her feelings down and turned off the machine, so the next two calls the phone just rang. Then she took the phone off the hook for a while. She thought, *Maybe now he will get the message.*

The next morning was the same, so she just took the phone off the hook. Katheryn figured she could transfer to a school at home and be perfectly fine with a master's half-Oxford, half-somewhere else. She would put this in motion today. She was going home. She started packing.

Over the next few days Katheryn ignored Jonathan's calls, his flowers, and his knocks on the door. She was not going back; she was going forward. Jonathan tried to talk to Charles, but all he could get him to say was "It really looked bad, Jonathan."

Jonathan thought, *If she doesn't talk to me, how will I ever explain to her?* Jonathan thought it would be best to give her a couple of days to think, and then he would try again.

Katheryn picked up her bag and checked for her passport. She looked around to make sure she had everything she was taking. She had asked Charles to mail the rest for her, which he was glad to do.

Charles knocked on the door. Katheryn made sure it was him. Charles took her luggage, and she followed. The car was packed, Katheryn looked around and said, "You are really nice, Oxford, but I am going home now." On the way to the airport, there was a sudden sadness that came over her. She didn't get to do and see the places she wanted to, but God-willing she would come back one day.

Chapter 22

Jonathan took the steps by twos leading up to Katheryn's flat. When he got to her door it was open; he walked in and called Katheryn's name. Charles answered, "Hi, Jonathan, she is not here."

Jonathan asked, "Where is she, Charles?"

Charles took a deep breath and said, "She has gone back to the United States."

Jonathan sat down, looked at Charles, and asked, "Why? Was it because of me?"

Charles said, "I really think it was a combination of things, to tell you the truth."

Jonathan kept saying "But it wasn't my fault."

Charles asked Jonathan, if he didn't mind, to tell him why he was there that day with that girl in the first place. Jonathan said, "She asked me to come and meet with several people to discuss what to get one of our professors that is retiring, but she was the only one there. I know it looked bad, but I swear I was trying to get away from her. She lied and she set me up. But I know one thing for sure, she will not be taking my place next year. I took care of that today." Jonathan held out his hand and said, "It has been a pleasure to know you, Charles."

Charles shook hands with Jonathan and said, "Yes, sir, it has been a privilege to know you and Katheryn."

Jonathan said, "What am I to do, Charles?"

Charles answered Jonathan, saying, "I would give her some time, but not too long, and I would write her a long letter explaining."

"Good luck, Jonathan."

Jonathan thanked Charles and left. As he walked down the steps all he could see was Katheryn laughing and telling him, in her beautiful Southern way of speaking, how great it was here when it didn't rain. He missed her, and it hurt in the pit of his stomach. His mind raced with questions and decisions. He thought about Katheryn's birthday; in just a week she would be twenty-three. And in a few more weeks he would be finished with his work and ready to take on his own class. And Katheryn wasn't here to celebrate with him, and he wasn't with her to celebrate her birthday. Jonathan was trying to think of what his father always said, *Oh, yes, he remembered, life can turn on a dime.* Well, his just did.

Katheryn got home and told Grand everything, Grand was so disappointed in Jonathan O'Conner. She was sure there must be more to the situation than what she knew. After a good cry, Grand sent Katheryn to bed for rest. Emilia's mind was really trying to get wrapped around this break between Jonathan and Katheryn. She thought, *I really need to take time to think about this clearly and objectively. I thought they were meant for each other, and I still do.* Emilia shook her head and said, "We will just have to wait and see what happens to this calamity!"

They had a small gathering for Katheryn's twenty-third birthday because she wanted it that way. There was no Emerson or Nancy. Just a few close friends. The next day Emilia and Katheryn met with the attorney to discuss her trust. Katheryn and Emilia sat in the attorney's office and listened to him read her father's words. As Katheryn and Emilia walked out of the attorney's office, Emilia said to Katheryn, "You are now a wealthy woman in your own right."

Katheryn was stunned when she looked at how much her trust was; it was unbelievable. Her father took well care of her, and she was thankful. She was still in shock when they arrived at home. Katheryn told Grand she would always be wise with her inheritance because it was her father's gift. Grand said, "I have no doubt you will. You know you are your father's child, my love." Katheryn smiled at her great-grandmother.

Katheryn decided to take some time off and work on her master's in January, go in second semester. Now she needed to decide where to finish her master's. She knew she could get into

Princeton easily because she had already applied there and was accepted. Okay, Princeton it is. After that decision was made, Katheryn felt free; she could breathe and leave the past behind. She still thought of Jonathan every day, but he betrayed her and that was unacceptable. It had been and still was very painful. She had loved him, and if she would admit the truth, she still did. She gave her heart away, and now it was broken; she needed time just to heal.

Katheryn's leg was doing great, but she still couldn't ride a bike or take a nice run. "Just a few more months," the doctor kept saying. So she would take long walks and swim.

The first of April, Katheryn told Emilia she wanted to hike a trial in the mountains. Somewhere on the Appalachian Trail. Grand said, "Katheryn, I think it is too soon. You need to ask the doctor first."

The next day Katheryn made an appointment with her doctor for a week later. She was still on the cane when her leg was tired. A week later she went to her appointment, and after an X-ray she sat in the room waiting on the doctor. Finally he came in and sat down.

"Ms, Kensington, your leg is healing beautifully. In about three or four months you can start getting back to some of your activities, but as far a running, skiing, riding a bike, and walking up mountains, you will have to wait for about four to six more months."

Katheryn looked at the doctor and said, "You have talked to Emilia Wardlaw Kensington, haven't you!"

The doctor smiled and answered, "Yes, ma'am, I have, but I am telling you the truth. This particular fracture needs time, and I promise you one day, in the not so far future, you will be running again."

Katheryn smiled and said, "Thank you." She made her next appointment and walked out the door, saying in a low voice, "The only good thing about this doctor visit is the fact he was absolutely gorgeous!" Katheryn thought, *My doctor visits are looking promising.* Then she thought of Jonathan and how handsome he was and that she could not believe he would cheat on her. He was the perfect gentleman, so intelligent, but most of all she loved him and she knew or thought he loved her though they had not yet spoken those words. Katheryn shook her head to clear it. *I can't think about him now, or I will cry.*

When Katheryn got home Grand and Rose were sitting out on the veranda having tea. Katheryn looked down at her watch, and it said it was five minutes after three. She thought, *Oops, I am five minutes late.* Emilia looked at her as she walked in and smiled, then she said, "You are late, my dear." Katheryn told Grand it was due to the gorgeous doctor she saw. Emilia smiled at her great-granddaughter then said, "I know, my dear, met him at the club. I thought Anna Lee Ferguson was going to drop her partial in her plate after he said hello to her."

Katheryn died out laughing and said, "No! That would have been hysterical! I would have had to leave the room." All three women were wiping tears from their eyes.

Katheryn poured her tea and sat down trying to get the image out of her mind of Anna Lee Ferguson and her partial. Katheryn looked at her great-grandmother and announced that she had an idea about the summer. Rose and Grand both said, "Do tell."

Katheryn continued to explain to the them summer was approaching and wouldn't it be nice to be by the sea for that time. Emilia said, "What a splendid idea. Where? Hilton Head, Charleston? We still have our summer home on Jekyll Island, and you always love going there, Katheryn."

Katheryn said, "Jekyll Island it is. I love Jekyll Island! So many great memories, Grand."

Grand said to Rose and Katheryn, "Well, that is settled, we will make plans."

Katheryn went into the house and walked into the foyer to see if she had any messages that were always laying on the beautiful round antique table in the middle of the foyer. There were a new bouquet of flowers and several messages. She was looking for one in particular, correspondence from Princeton University. Katheryn thought, not yet, but it was still early. She looked at flowers. They were beautiful, and they were from Jonathan. She read the card, and it said, "Please talk to me, Katheryn. Love, Jonathan."

There was also a letter from him she would not open. She couldn't; he broke her heart. She dropped it back onto the table and left it. Grand walked up and said, "What is this? Oh, Katheryn, shouldn't you at least read what the poor young man has to say?"

Katheryn answered her great-grandmother with moist eyes. "I can't. He broke my heart, Grand."

Emilia said, "It is okay. I will keep it for you, and maybe one day you would want to read it."

Katheryn walked away, saying, "I doubt it, Grand." What Katheryn didn't know was Grand was keeping all letters and cards coming from Jonathan that she discarded. Emilia wanted them to be there in case one day she might change her mind.

The next day she received her acceptance letter from Princeton. Now Katheryn was all set for January to start completing her master's. Katheryn found Grand and explained she got her letter from Princeton and everything was set for January. Emilia was so pleased and happy to see a smile on Katheryn's face where there had not been one for a while. All three women—Katheryn, Emilia, and Rose—decided to celebrate with cocktails on the veranda, and they could also start making their plans for their trip to Jekyll Island.

Chapter 23

Jekyll Island was every bit as beautiful as Katheryn remembered. The house was lovely with all windows open to the sea. The salt air had a wonderful healing force. Katheryn walked down to the beach and just let her senses completely take over the beauty, sounds, and wonderful smells of the sea. The thought of Jonathan flickered through her mind against her will, she said out loud to herself, "You would really have liked it here, Jonathan." With tears in her eyes she turned and walked back up to the house saddened by the fact that he had crept into her mind once again.

Emilia stood on the porch watching her great-granddaughter and could tell by the look on her face she was in pain. Although Emilia thought about writing Jonathan several times, she didn't; she did not want to cross that line. She waited to hear from him first.

Katheryn walked up the steps to the porch and spotted Grand. Her mood changed instantly. "Hey, Grand, what a beautiful day!"

Emilia smiled at her Katheryn and agreed with her that is was a lovely day. Emilia watched Katheryn walk through with her head down. Emilia knew she was thinking about him and wished she could help her. It was sad to say, but this kind of thing, one had to go through on their own.

Katheryn went through and up to her room, closed the door, and laid across her bed. She just let the tears flow. Rose heard Katheryn sobbing as she walked by her room. She started to say something, but she decided the girl needed some time to herself. Rose met Emilia on the porch. Rose told Emilia she is in her room crying and that she felt so bad for her. Emilia agreed and said, "These things take time.

When she comes through it, she will be stronger for it." Rose agreed. They both just sat in silence watching the waves hit the beach and thought about their girl.

Their summer was wonderful and quiet. Katheryn would take long walks on the beach, all three caught up on their reading, and it was just what they needed. On their last night they made a low country boil, which consisted of shrimp, corn on cob, sausage, onion, and potatoes. As Katheryn looked at her plate, she said, "Oh, how I have missed this!" All in agreement, it was delicious, and they were so glad this was their tradition. Last night would always be a low county boil.

With everything wrap up at the summer home the next day, they left midmorning and headed back to Abbeville, South Carolina. Emilia was looking forward to getting home to get ready for the fall festivities. Katheryn was thinking about what she would do to keep busy until January. She was looking forward to being released from the doctor where she could do some more activities other than swimming.

When they got home there was a huge stack of mail. Katheryn walked right past the mail without even looking. Emilia looked at her with sadness and just shook her head. After they were settled in, Emilia decided to go through the mail. As she was flipping through, she noticed a letter from Jonathan O'Conner addressed to her. Emilia looked around to see if she was alone. She took the letter to the Carolina room, where it was cool, and sat down. She opened the letter and started to read. She was surprised and elated all at the same time. Jonathan asked her not to reveal to Katheryn his intentions and what he was going to do. Jonathan did explain the fact that he was set up by the girl and he was trying to get away from her, but Katheryn would not hear him and he was heartbroken over the entire ordeal. She heard Katheryn coming, so she hid the letter under her cushion on her seat. Katheryn walked into the Carolina room and asked Emilia if there was anything important in the mail. Emilia said, "I am not sure, dear, I just started going through it." Then she asked Katheryn if she would help.

Katheryn said, "Sure." She took a large stack of mail and started looking through making piles.

She came across three letters from Jonathan. She looked up at Grand and said, "Will he ever leave me alone? Why does he keep writing me, Grand?"

Emilia looked at her great-granddaughter with kindness and said, "Katheryn, sometime you may need to read his letters to have an understanding. Maybe there is something you do not know or maybe not. But it might be good idea to read a few and then make your decision to throw them all away or not. You really haven't given it a chance to be part of your healing."

Katheryn looked at Emilia and said, "Maybe you are right, Grand." Emilia told Katheryn she had all the letters she had thrown away, and when she wanted to read them to just let her know. Katheryn knew she should, but right now it was too painful. She got up and said, "Maybe later, Grand. It just hurts too much right now."

Katheryn walked out of the room, and Emilia thought, *One day she really needs to read these letters. I think the poor child would be surprised.*

Chapter 24

Katheryn pained through the seasons with Grand, Christmas and New Year's. Her heart just wasn't into anything but getting ready to go to Princeton, get her degree, and then maybe travel for a while. She tried picking up her research on the ring but lost interest; she just couldn't concentrate on it because it reminded her of Jonathan. Her leg was great, and she was running everyday building up her strength. She was trying to get back into her life and have some normalcy. She even dated a few times during the holidays, but her heart just wasn't into it. Maybe she would meet someone new at Princeton, she hoped.

At least that pain in the pit of her stomach was gone now, but she still wasn't ready to read Jonathan's letters even though they kept coming.

Katheryn said goodbye to her dear Grand and decided to drive up to New Jersey. She had plenty of time to get settled in her new apartment before her classes started. She could stop on the way and visit the little fishing villages scattered all along the coast. She set off on her journey with a fresh new outlook, hoping this was a new turn in her path.

The first place Katheryn stopped was a quaint little town called Southport in North Carolina. She found a charming bed-and-breakfast facing the ocean within walking distance to all the cute little shops. She spent the night in a wonderful room with a beautiful high poster bed and gorgeous antiques.

The next morning the breakfast was delicious, and the proprietors were so nice and friendly. She was so glad she had stopped in Southport. On her way again, she wondered what other cute towns lay ahead of her.

As Katheryn drove north the temperature kept dropping. Every time she stopped she could feel it getting colder. When she hit the Washington area, it started to snow. Her jeep had four-wheel drive, so she was not worried but it was coming down so hard she couldn't see well. Katheryn knew she needed to stop, but where? Her map was not helping at the moment. People were starting to pull over and taking ramps to areas that might have a hotel she was sure. Katheryn thought she saw a sign for a hotel, so she took the next ramp off the highway. It was now snowing so hard, she could not see a thing. She just pulled her car into what she thought was a parking lot. She grabbed the throw that Grand gave her lying in the back seat. It was made of wool, and she was hoping it would keep her warm. Katheryn wrapped herself up in the blanket and just sat in the car, there was nothing else she could do but watch it snow. She had some coffee and snacks from her last stop, so she would be okay. She was so glad Grand made her take the thermos because it now held hot coffee. After a while Katheryn dosed off to sleep.

She was awakened in the morning by an officer knocking on her window asking if she was okay. She could only see through the small hole the officer had made to see into her car. "Miss, are you all right?" asked the officer.

Katheryn answered, "I think so."

The officer tried to open her door, and she tried to help. The officer finally got Katheryn's driver-side door open. "Hi, I am Officer Ryan Wardlaw. We need to get you out of this car."

Katheryn grabbed her backpack—it had everything she needed in it—and slid out the door with the officer's help. As she looked around she could not believe she was sitting in a field in the middle of nowhere. Katheryn looked at the officer and asked, "Where am I?" He told her she was in Virginia but very close to Washington DC.

Officer Wardlaw explained to Katheryn, "We need to get you warm. Let's get you into my truck." Katheryn thought the truck was so warm, and it felt so good; her feet were frozen. The officer closed Katheryn's door and walked around to the driver's side and got into the truck and called someone to pull Katheryn's jeep out of the snowbank. Officer Wardlaw turned to Katheryn and asked her, "Where were you going, and do you have a place to stay?"

Katheryn answered, "I was going to Princeton, and no, I do not have a place to stay."

Officer Wardlaw said the roads are closed but should be open soon and that he lived right down the road. He told her she was welcome to go there for a while until the roads are cleared. Katheryn said, "Thank you, and I think you and I might be related. I am Katheryn Wardlaw Kensington."

Officer Ryan Wardlaw said, "Nice to meet you".

The house down the street turned out to be a huge white farmhouse with a wraparound porch in a beautiful setting with large snow-covered trees; it was breathtaking. Officer Ryan and Katheryn came in a side door with the steps cleared from the snow. They walked into what looked like a small room with boots lined up and coats hanging on hooks and benches. Officer Ryan sat down and took off his shoes. Katheryn did the same, but her feet were freezing. Officer Ryan pulled out a drawer, got a pair of socks, and handed them to her. They walked through into a large kitchen. There were two people standing at a window drinking coffee. Katheryn thought it smelled so good. Ryan said, "Mom, Dad, I would like for you to meet Katheryn Wardlaw Kensington. Katheryn, my parents, Mary and Donald Wardlaw."

They both immediately came to her rescue. They were the sweetest people Katheryn had met in a long time. There was a beautiful fireplace in the kitchen with a roaring fire. Katheryn commented to the Ryans, "Your home is beautiful."

Mary answered her, "Thank you, my dear. It has been in the Wardlaw family for a long time."

Mr. Wardlaw chimed in, "Four generations. Where are you from?"

Katheryn explained some of her background as Mary set a plate of food down on the bar and said, "You need to eat, sweetie." Katheryn told them about her ancestors coming in from Scotland and settling in Virginia but relocating to Abbeville, South Carolina, due to the British during the Revolutionary War. She went on to tell them that Abbeville was full of Wardlaws, alive and dead.

Donald Wardlaw said, "I have heard stories from my relatives about that era. We are most likely related."

Katheryn said with a smile, "Who would have thought on my drive to Princeton I would get into a snowstorm and meet family? God is good." They all talked and exchanged numbers and made promises to visit. Ryan got a call. Katheryn's car was fine, and they would drop it by Ryan's in about thirty minutes. As Katheryn warmed herself she thought she was glad she got to meet each one of them; they were kind people, and their farm was impressive.

Katheryn learned that Ryan was one of three children; he had two sisters. Although he was an officer he would one day take over the farm. Katheryn thought, *Ryan's life was already mapped out, and oddly, he seems fine with it and even looks forward to it.* Katheryn could see that they had a large business, and it looked to be a very prosperous one. Katheryn looked at Ryan and thought he was the most handsome man she had ever seen; he was actually beautiful. His hair was dark, almost black, and he had the bluest eyes she had ever seen. Why, his eyes were gorgeous! He must have a girlfriend; no wife because she did not see a ring on his finger. Mary was saying something. Katheryn said, "I am sorry, I was a million miles away thinking about this beautiful place."

Mary smiled and said, "I was just asking what you were majoring in at Princeton."

"Oh," Katheryn replied, "I am working on my master's in history." Mary told Katheryn that was wonderful and that she had two daughters, one taught senior high English and the other one taught Math to six graders and they both loved it. Ryan announced to Katheryn her car was here, and she asked how much was the cost.

Ryan said, "Nothing, don't worry about it, just neighbor helping neighbor."

Katheryn looked at all three and said with a thankful heart, "Thank you all for a lovely morning, and I will definitely visit again if you will have me."

They all chimed in to tell her that she was welcome anytime. Ryan walked Katheryn out to her car, and after she was safely in, he said, "It was a pleasure to meet you, Katheryn."

Katheryn smiled and replied, "It was a pleasure to meet you too and your precious parents. Goodbye, Ryan."

Ryan said, "Goodbye and take care."

Chapter 25

Emilia sat by the fireplace reading Jonathan's latest letter. He was doing very well, had taken a professorship at an Ivy League University for a year, and was looking forward to lecturing again. He wanted to visit Katheryn, even though she didn't want to see him, but so much was going on trying to accomplish his task at hand. He couldn't believe it had been ten months since he had last seen her. Of course he wanted to know how she was and what she was doing. Emilia had to be very selective on what she wrote to Jonathan about Katheryn; she didn't want Katheryn to think she had betrayed her.

That could be disastrous, so she had to avoid certain areas of information. Emilia thought, *I am so deep in this already. I am sure Katheryn would not be pleased with me.* Emilia laid the letter in her lap and spoke to Rose, "She should be settled in her apartment now, thank heavens for those wonderful people and being Wardlaws to boot! And with Katheryn going through that horrible snowstorm, which could have turn out very badly, I might add."

Rose spoke up and said, "Yes, thank God for taking care of her. She is a strong young woman, and I do think she is in a good place mentally now. I believe she will be fine." Emilia agreed with her dear friend Rose, knowing how much Rose loved Katheryn too.

At the same time Emilia and Rose were having their conversation about Katheryn, she was putting the finishing touches in her new apartment. The movers brought in everything she and Grand had bought earlier. The apartment looked great, and she loved her fireplace. She had decided she would always have a fireplace wherever she lived. Her class would start next week, and this weekend Officer Ryan was coming to visit. She had called his mom to thank her again and to get an address to send flowers. She left her number with Mary and asked her to please call her anytime. Then Ryan called. They made a date for this weekend, and he would stay with her. She would put him in the guest bedroom with his own bathroom, so in her mind it would work out nicely. She was looking forward to seeing Ryan; he was such a gentleman and wasn't bad to look at either. Katheryn wanted everything to be perfect before he got here tomorrow afternoon. Katheryn calculated. It would take him approximately three and half hours to get there, so from the time he told her he was leaving he should arrive just in time for dinner. She would make something good and easy like a casserole with a nice salad. This was the first time in a long time Katheryn was actually looking forward to something with heightened anticipation. She decided to call Grand and tell her about Ryan. She dialed the number, and the maid answered.

"Hey, Charlotte, this is Katheryn. Is Grand there?"

Charlotte said, "Yes, she is, I will get her."

Grand picked up the phone, saying, "Hello, my dear child, how are you? And we all miss you!" Katheryn told Grand she was great, the apartment looked wonderful, her class would start next week, and asked her to guess who is coming to dinner. Grand said, "Tell me, I cannot stand the suspense, my dear."

Katheryn said, "Well, the one and only Officer Ryan Wardlaw."

Grand answered, "Really, tell me more."

Katheryn told Grand all about Ryan and how handsome he was and he had the most beautiful blue eyes. Then Katheryn blurted out with heightened emotion and anticipation, "Grand, I am so excited, 1996 is looking up!" Emilia told her she was so happy for her and she couldn't wait to hear all the news of his visit.

Katheryn had to run errands, so she told Grand she loved her and she would call soon and let her know how her date went. The phone went dead, and Emilia was still holding the phone to her ear, thinking, *She is moving on. Poor Jonathan.* Emilia's next thought was, *Rose and I might need to pay a visit to Princeton, and it should be fairly soon.*

Katheryn was applying the final touches to her table before Ryan arrived. The doorbell rang, and she jumped. She needed a glass wine to calm her jitters. She opened the door, and there stood this incredibly handsome man with flowers in his hand with a beautiful smile on his face. Ryan said, "Hello."

Katheryn smiled and said, "Hello, please come in, Officer Wardlaw."

Ryan handed her the flowers, and she went to get a vase. Ryan looked around her apartment and said, "Nice place, Katheryn."

She thanked him and took his coat and asked him to bring his bag and follow her. Katheryn led him to the guest bedroom and got him settled. She asked Ryan if he was hungry, and he answered, "Always."

She told him, "Good."

They returned to the kitchen. Katheryn poured two glasses of wine. They picked their glasses up, and Ryan said, "To our first date."

Katheryn smiled and said, "To our first date."

They had a great time through the entire weekend. They laughed and got to know each other.

Katheryn thought he was very sweet, attentive, and so comfortable to be with. Before he left he leaned down and kissed her, first on her forehead, then he kissed her on the mouth slowly then deeper. He then pulled away and whispered, "Katheryn, it has been a pleasure," and then he kissed her again, and Katheryn knew she would always remember it took her breath away. Ryan held her and said he didn't want to go.

She held on to him and said, "I know."

Finally, he kissed her on top her head and said, "I will see you soon, and I will call you when I get home." He kissed her once more and left.

After Katheryn closed the door, she smiled and thought, *What a great weekend with a wonderful guy. I do believe I have moved on.* As she sat by the fire with a glass of wine she thought about all they did and what they talked about. He was funny and sweet. She missed him already. When she was in bed the phone rang, and she knew it was Ryan; he was home and safe. They agreed they would talk tomorrow. Ryan said, "Sweet dreams, Katheryn."

She whispered, "Good night, Ryan."

Chapter 26

On Tuesday morning, Katheryn ran over to the university to find the building where her first class would be the next day, to be prepared. She was in hope of finishing her master's as soon as possible. As she ran back to her apartment, feeling good about her leg she previously broke, she thought about Grand's conversation earlier this morning. She seemed a little off, talking about coming up to see her. Grand doesn't particularly like to travel in the winter, and it was so cold here. Katheryn thought she might call Rose to make sure Grand was okay. She stopped at a coffee shop adjacent to her apartment, which was really convenient, and they made the most delicious coffee. While she waited for her coffee, she took out her new cell phone that she absolutely loved and dialed home. The maid answered, and she asked for Rose. The maid said, "Just a moment." Katheryn grabbed her coffee and walked out of the coffee shop still waiting for Rose to come to the phone.

Rose finally answered, "Hello, this is Rose Stevens."

Katheryn said, "Hey, Rose, it's Katheryn."

Rose answered, "How are you, my dear?"

Katheryn told her she was fine, but she had a concern about Grand. Katheryn conveyed her concerns to Rose, but Rose assured her Grand was fine. Katheryn said, "Thank you. I love you, Rose."

Rose said, "I love you, baby girl."

After their goodbyes, Katheryn felt better, but something still seemed a little off.

What took Rose so long to get to the phone call from Katheryn was because she was already in the car ready to go to the airport. When Rose got back into the car she looked at Emilia and said, "Baby girl knows something is up, what did you say to her?"

Emilia thought over her last conversation with Katheryn and couldn't think of anything she might have said that would cause any alarm. Emilia said to Rose, "I do not think I said anything to alert her."

Rose looked at Emilia and said, "We have got to be careful, Emilia. She suspects something. She thinks you are ill, which could be the truth with all your shenanigans!"

Both women died out laughing. Emilia kept saying, "True, oh so true."

Rose and Emilia discussed their strategy on the plane. They would get to their hotel, get settled, and surprise Katheryn with a phone call or a visit. Of course, when they would do this they had not figured out as of yet. Rose just kept saying, "I know there is trouble coming, I just know it!" Emilia would pat Rose's hand and tell her everything would be fine. Rose was not convinced.

When Emilia and Rose finally got settled into their hotel suite, it was approaching late evening. They both agreed it would scare Katheryn to death if they called her at this time so late, therefore they decided to call in the morning or surprise her with a visit. They would decide later.

The next morning, Katheryn was up and ready to go at eight in the morning, her class started at nine forty-five, and she wanted a good seat. She made sure she left her cell phone in the off position and dropped it in her backpack. Katheryn stopped by the coffee shop and then took a leisurely walk to her class. Just before she walked into her building, she stopped and knocked the snow off her boots. She entered the building, walked down the hall, and turned right; her class was the first door on the right. There was a man changing names and class times on the information board. She glanced over to make sure her time was still the same, and it was. She walked into the class, found a seat a couple of rows back, and sat down. She was looking forward to this class because she had not been able to finish it at Oxford due to her accident. The room was filling up and looked to be a full class with no seats remaining. Katheryn had her pens and paper ready for notes. Someone behind her said, "I am so lucky I got into this guy's class. From what I have heard his lectures are outstanding."

Katheryn thought, *Good, this should be an interesting class.* A little after nine forty-five, the professor walked in and shut the door. His back was to Katheryn, and she could not see his face. The professor walked up to the board and wrote his name. Katheryn moved her body so she could have a better view. She could see the name O'Conner on the board. Katheryn thought, *Great, I cannot get away from that name.* The professor turned and began to talk. Katheryn's heart felt like it would jump out of her chest. She couldn't speak. She quickly scanned the room. There was no easy way out of the room without everyone seeing her including Jonathan. Katheryn thought, *Oh my god, what am I going to do? Why is he here?* She started to shake, and then everything went black.

One of her classmates yelled, "Hey, this chick just passed out!"

Jonathan looked up at the guy yelling and then down to the girl. Jonathan yelled, "Call for help."

He ran up the steps to the girl and told the class to move away from her and give her room to breathe. Jonathan pulled the girl up slightly and laid her back into his arms with one of his hands cradling her neck. When he saw the girl's face his heart exploded with fear. He felt her pulse, and it was faint. "Don't you do this to me, Katheryn! Katheryn, can you hear me?" He pulled his hand from the back of her neck to get a better hold on her in his arms, and there was blood on his hand. He just held her close until the EMTs got there.

Finally, the EMTs arrived. They accessed her, then they laid her on a gurney, and moving quickly, they loaded her in the ambulance. As they were getting ready to take her away Jonathan yelled, "What hospital?"

The guy yelled back, "St. Francis."

Jonathan's class was almost over anyway, so he handed out an assignment, dismissed his class, and headed out to the hospital.

Emilia and Rose were at Katheryn's apartment. They both stayed in the car while the driver went to see if she was at home. The driver came back and said, "No answer at the door, I knocked several times."

Emilia took out her cell and handed it to Rose to call Katheryn. Rose called Katheryn's cell several times, but there was no answer. Emilia asked, "Where could she be, Rose?"

Rose just shook her head and mumbled, "I don't know, maybe school." They left not knowing Katheryn was on her way to the hospital with Jonathan in tow.

Emilia and Rose went back to the hotel to wait and call Katheryn again. She still did not answer her phone, the one at the apartment and her cell. Emilia had an uneasy feeling, and so did Rose. They both jumped when the phone rang. Rose picked the phone and said, "Hello, Katheryn, is that you?" But it wasn't Katheryn; it was their maid from home.

Rose looked at Emilia and said, "It is Renee!"

Emilia said, "What does she want?"

Rose was trying to hear Renee but couldn't for Emilia questions. Rose told Renee to hold and looked at Emilia and said, "You have got to be quiet, where I can hear what she is saying, Emilia!"

Emilia agreed, "Okay."

Rose told Renee she could continue. Rose was frantically asking, "Where did they take her?"

Renee said, "St. Francis Hospital."

Rose said, "Thank you, Renee, we will keep you updated."

Emilia was going crazy, and Rose was calling for the car. Rose said to Emilia, "Katheryn collapsed at school, and they have taken her by ambulance to St. Francis Hospital. Jonathan is with her, and he was the one that called Renee with the information to tell us. He did not know we were here, but he does now." Rose and Emilia started praying for Katheryn.

Jonathan was sitting in the waiting room waiting for someone to tell him how Katheryn was and what was going on. He decided to get something to drink. He spotted a vending machine at the end of waiting room and got a cup of tea. After he tasted it, he dropped it into the trash. He went back and sat down. After a few minutes he heard a voice that he knew. He looked down the hall and saw Emilia and Rose. He smiled in wonder at these two elderly gracious women and their stamina. Emilia threw her arms in the air and then clasped her hands and said to Jonathan, "Bless your heart, my sweet boy, but we need to find another place to meet besides a hospital! How is our girl?"

Jonathan shook his head and said, "I do not know anything."

Emilia hugged Jonathan, and so did Rose. Emilia said, "You come with me, darling, and we will find out." Then she grabbed Jonathan's hand. Emilia gracefully asked the lady at the desk about Katheryn Wardlaw Kensington and told her that Katheryn was her great-granddaughter. Emilia asked the lady in a way that would motivate a person to find out as much as they could and as quickly as possible. Emilia turned and said to Rose and Jonathan, "We should know something soon."

They all went over to sit down and waited for the lady to come back with some news, but instead, a doctor came into the waiting room and asked for the Kensington family. All three stood up, and Emilia said, "Here we are."

The doctor introduced himself as Dr. Morgan and asked if they would follow him, and they did. He led them into an area closed off for privacy. The doctor asked if they could give him a little background on Katheryn. Emilia started then turned it over to Jonathan. Jonathan explained about the train wreck, the concussion, broken leg, and coma. Jonathan also told the doctor that his father worked at the hospital in England and was Katheryn's doctor. Jonathan continued to convey to Dr. Morgan that all the medical information he needed he could get from his father.

The doctor said, "Good, good, this is a big help. At the present time we are running extensive test including an MRI. She hasn't awakened yet, but we do have her on a mild sedative. Did anything happen, a trauma of some sorts?"

Jonathan said, "We were together after her accident. We were a couple. Something happened that she thought was really something else, but it wasn't. She saw a girl kiss me, but she didn't see me trying to get away from the girl. It was a ploy for someone to obtain a position at my university; of course it didn't work. Katheryn and I were separated for a while because of this unfortunate act of a demented person. I applied for a temporary professorship position here at Princeton, got the position, and this was my first day. It was also Katheryn's first day here as a grad student. She was in my class. Evidently, she didn't know I was her professor. When she saw me she collapsed. I do not think it was seeing me. I think there is a problem, but seeing me might have brought it on. Also, when I held her, her head was bleeding."

The doctor said, "You might be on to something. Yes, this is why we are doing an MRI. This gives me a clearer picture of the situation, and I would like to have the information on how to get in touch with your father."

Jonathan said, "Absolutely."

Dr. Morgan handed paper and pen to Jonathan. Jonathan wrote down all his father's information and handed it back to the doctor. Emilia and Rose offered anything they could, and also, Emilia wanted to know if they could see her. Dr. Morgan said maybe later, but he would allow them to see her through the window in ICU now. Dr. Morgan also added she was sedated and they were giving her fluids and of course running test. Dr. Morgan turned to Jonathan and said, "Mr. O'Conner, I will call your father now. I think it is imperative." They all went to ICU to look through a window at Katheryn, and when they saw her all three cried.

They all went to the ICU waiting room to decide what to do until the doctor could get all the results back and figure out what is wrong with Katheryn. Jonathan sat with his head in his hands while Emilia patted him on the shoulder. Rose kept rolling a handkerchief around with her hands. They all three were distraught. The nurse came over and asked if there was a Jonathan O'Conner. Jonathan held his hand up to show her it was him. She said, "Sir, you have a phone call from England. Please follow me." Jonathan followed the nurse to an office area. The nurse picked up the phone and handed it to Jonathan, then she left the room.

Jonathan said, "Hello."

The man who answered was his father. Dr. O'Conner asked his son how he was holding up.

Jonathan said in a broken voice and desperately trying to not to show the emotion he felt, "Father, I don't think it is good. Something is wrong."

Dr. O'Conner was one of those rare Englishmen who thought you should show your emotions; he said it was healthy, and he contributed it to his Irish heritage. Dr. O'Conner said, "Jonathan, if you need to cry, cry. I am booked on the next flight out, and I will see you soon, son. I love you."

Dr. O'Conner knew what Katheryn meant to Jonathan, and he knew he loved her. Jonathan, said, "Thank you, Dad. Be safe. I love you."

Jonathan went back to Emilia and Rose with news his father was coming. Emilia and Rose both were so thankful; they thought any help at this point would be a bonus. They were all touched by the fact that Dr. O'Conner would be actually here in a short while.

Dr. Morgan walked into the ICU waiting room and explained that he was looking forward to meeting Jonathan's father. Dr. Morgan said, "Dr. O'Conner has been published too many times to count, and I have the utmost respect for him."

Jonathan said, "Thank you."

Dr. Morgan told all three they needed to go home and rest, if there is any change he would call them immediately. They all agreed but wanted one more look at Katheryn. Dr. Morgan said, "Absolutely."

They all walked into ICU together, and Dr. Morgan explained everything they were doing, then he left promising to stay in touch. He had all their numbers.

As they walked out of the hospital, Jonathan turned to Emilia to tell her he had Katheryn's backpack. He had taken out her school credentials, driver's license, and gave them to the EMT. Emilia said, "Jonathan, will you please just hang onto Katheryn's possessions for me?"

He said, "Of course."

Jonathan kept her things with him; somehow it made him feel closer to her. Jonathan had a townhouse near the school where a lot of the professors lived, but he hated the thought of being alone tonight. Emilia noticed and said, "Jonathan, would you mind staying with two old ladies? We have a wonderful suite with four bedrooms."

Jonathan said, "It would be an honor. I will just run by my townhouse and pick up a few things and meet you there."

The ladies said, "Wonderful, see you soon."

Jonathan went home, packed a suitcase, and sat down to pray for Katheryn. He was so close to his goal, and she had to be all right. She was his love. After he finished praying, he left to be with Emilia and Rose.

Chapter 27

Jonathan cancelled his classes and rescheduled. His schedule now was open for the next week. Jonathan got settled in his room at the suite then went to meet the ladies in the common area to say good night. They all needed a good night's sleep.

The next morning all three met in the common area. There was a maid taking care of everything. Jonathan sat down at the table and asked for hot tea. Surprisingly, it was very good. He had part of a muffin and got up to leave. Emilia said, "Jonathan, you need more than that."

He picked up a piece of bacon and smiled at Emilia. He told them he would go on over to the hospital because he was sure his father was already there. The ladies said they would come later. Jonathan said if there was any slight change he would call. He took out Katheryn's cell phone and said, "I have her cell phone, so if you need me, call."

Jonathan arrived at the hospital. He went straight to ICU. He walked into ICU area where he was able to look through the window to see Katheryn and saw his father and Dr. Morgan talking and looking over Katheryn's chart. They looked serious, and it scared him. He stood there watching them with what seemed a long time, but in reality it was only minutes. The two doctors came out of the room, and Dr. Morgan shook Jonathan's hand then told him his father would fill him in. Dr. O'Conner said to his son, "Let's find a quiet place to talk, son. By the way, it is good to see you." Dr. O'Conner put his arm around Jonathan's shoulder but didn't say a word until they sat down.

Dr. O'Conner started to bring Jonathan up to date. He said, "Her MRI was negative, so that is good news. After some other test results came in, we think Katheryn has neurocardiogenic syncope, which is a sudden drop in heart rate and blood pressure leading to fainting, often due to a reaction to something stressful. We can treat this very nicely with medication. She will have a tilt table test today, which will confirm our findings. She is awake; we still have her on a light sedative. In my judgment, this is what it is, and trust me, she will be fine. She can lead a normal life with this, no problem."

Jonathan hugged his father and said, "You are the best father in the world! What about the blood coming from her head?"

Dr. O'Conner said, "Simply a flesh wound, that is all."

Jonathan was elated. They walked out together and ran into Emilia and Rose. Dr. O'Conner explained once again to the sweet ladies. Everyone was very grateful. Jonathan asked his father if had got a hotel yet, and he said no. The ladies said, "You will stay in our suite with us, don't say another word."

Jonathan said, "Dad, you are outnumbered." Jonathan took his father to the hotel to get some rest.

After his father was settled in his room, Jonathan walked out on to the balcony and looked across the college town. He decided that if Katheryn was all right he would leave Princeton and go home. He would not be the trigger that caused her problem. Katheryn's phone rang in his pocket. Jonathan answered it, "Hello, Katheryn Kensington's phone."

On the other end was Ryan Wardlaw. He said he had been trying to get in touch with Katheryn. Jonathan updated him on what had been going on. Ryan Wardlaw, in Jonathan's mind, seemed to be upset. Ryan asked what hospital she was in. Jonathan gave him the information, then they hung up.

They moved Katheryn to a regular room, and after she was settled Emilia and Rose were allowed to come in and sit with her.

Katheryn asked a million questions and asked where Jonathan was. Emilia said, "He is with his father, who by the way came all the way from

England to see about you at Jonathan's request. We were all worried sick, Katheryn."

Katheryn said, "He shouldn't have bothered."

Emilia had never been disappointed in her granddaughter until today. Emilia said, "I know you are in the hospital but will be out in a day or so. I know you have had a fright, but I have always taught you to be graceful, so now I expect you to be and especially to Dr. O'Conner since he is the one that found out what is wrong with you!"

Katheryn looked at Grand and said, "I am sorry, Grand, please forgive me. I wasn't expecting to see him again."

Grand said, "I don't think he was expecting to ever see you either. You know, Katheryn, what happened in Oxford with that girl was not Jonathan's fault! She wanted his job, and if you had waited to see what happened next, you could have saved yourself a lot of grief. He practically threw the girl away from him and told her she would never get a job at Oxford if he had anything to do with it. So if you had read his letters or even talked to him, you would know he loved you with all his heart."

As Grand finished the word *heart*, she turned to see a man standing with a bouquet of roses. Ryan wished he had not heard any of the conversation. He walked in and introduced himself and said, "I just stopped by to see how our patient was doing, heard you had a bad couple of days."

Katheryn just said, "Yes."

Emilia got up to leave with Rose and said, "I will leave you to your visit. I will see you tomorrow, my dear."

Then Emilia and Rose left. Katheryn felt awkward, and so did Ryan. He reached down to kiss her on her forehead and gave her the roses. She said, "Thank you, Ryan, but you should have not come all this way. I am fine."

Ryan said, "No problem."

He sat down and asked her what happened. She explained what she had and that she had fainted in class. Katheryn said she would be right as rain and it is regulated well with medication. Ryan said, "Wonderful, I called and called. Finally, some guy, really nice by the way, with an English accent, answered and filled me in on what happened to you and said you were in the hospital."

Katheryn asked, "Did he say anything else?"

Ryan told her, "No, he didn't."

Dr. Morgan came in to check on Katheryn and asked Ryan if they could have a moment. Ryan said, "Sure, I need to run anyway. Take care of her, Doc. See you soon, Katheryn." Then he left.

Dr. Morgan sat down in a chair and said, "I am waiting on Dr. O'Conner, and here he is, wonderful."

Dr. O'Conner walked up to Katheryn's bed and asked Katheryn, "How are you, my dear? It is good to see you again, but next time not in a hospital, okay?"

Katheryn smiled. Dr. Morgan and Dr. O'Conner explained to Katheryn what she had and that she would be fine, that with medication she could do anything she wanted. Dr. Morgan would keep a watch on her with check-ups, and Dr. O'Conner said, "For fear of repeating myself, you should be fine."

Katheryn asked a few questions but was sure they had explained everything quite nicely and thanked them. And especially thanked Dr. O'Conner for making a trip across the pond just for her. He answered her with "You are so welcome, my dear, and of course this also gave me a chance to visit with my son, even though I wished it had been better circumstances. Goodbye, Katheryn, take care."

Then both doctors left the room. Katheryn had a lot to think about that evening, with what Grand said and Ryan, and of course what Dr. Morgan and Dr. O'Conner said. She was troubled with a heavy heart. Jonathan came to her rescue once more.

Chapter 28

Jonathan sat with his dad on the plane. He looked over at his father and was glad to see he was sleeping peacefully. Jonathan could not believe his life just took a three-hundred-and-sixty-degree turn. He resigned from Princeton, and now he was going home. Jonathan had found out his mother was sick, and she was more important to him than any job. Jonathan took a deep breath and laid back in his seat and closed his eyes. The first thought that went through his mind was Katheryn. She looked really good, still as beautiful as ever, and she would always be his first love but he had to let her go. When he got settled at home he would gather all his research and send it to Emilia. He knew he could find a position in New Abbot or something close so he could be near his mother. He would always hope the best for Katheryn, but this chapter of his and Katheryn's book was closed.

While Jonathan was closing his and Katheryn's book, Katheryn was being discharged from the hospital. She knew Grand and Rose would be here soon to pick her up and take her home. She sat on the side of her bed with her discharge papers in her hand. Grand and Rose walked into her room. Grand asked, "Ready to go, my dear?"

Katheryn answered, "Yes, ma'am."

The nurse brought a wheelchair in for Katheryn. Katheryn asked, "Do I really have to?"

The nurse firmly said, 'Hospital policy, sorry." Katheryn gave in and sat down in the wheelchair, then they headed for the exit of the hospital to meet the car and go home. Emilia took Katheryn to her apartment. She and Rose helped her get settled. Emilia sent the driver to pick up her medicine and gave him a list of groceries to buy for her.

Emilia asked Katheryn, "Is there anything you might need, dear, before we go? Our flight is very early in the morning." Katheryn looked at Grand and Rose like they were deserting her. Grand asked, "Now you must think and tell me if there is anything you might need, dear?"

Katheryn said, "Grand, what is wrong? Why are you leaving so soon? Can we talk? Grand, I need to talk to you!"

Emilia looked at Katheryn and asked, "What do you want to talk about, dear?"

Katheryn started crying. Emilia had to hold herself back from putting her arms around her; sometimes tough love was the hardest thing you would ever do. Katheryn said, "I just need to talk." Grand and Rose sat down and waited to hear what she had to say. Katheryn asked, "Grand, do you still have Jonathan's letters?"

Emilia answered, "Yes, I do." Katheryn asked if she could have them. Emilia said, "Absolutely!" Katheryn wanted to know if they were at home in South Carolina. Emilia explained, "Actually they are here with me. I brought them with me just in case you might ask." Emilia asked Rose to call the driver and tell him to bring the blue box up.

In a few minutes, there was a knock at the door. Rose answered, and it was the driver with the blue box. Rose took the box and handed it to Katheryn. Emilia explained to her great-granddaughter that it would be best if she would read them in the order they came in and also all the cards. Emilia also explained to her that she had also placed the cards in the box that came with flowers. Katheryn looked at Grand with tears and said, "I have been a fool, haven't I?"

Emilia answered her with "There is always redemption, my sweet child, but it comes with a time limit."

Katheryn said, "I hope my time hasn't run out."

Emilia put her arm around her Katheryn and held her as she cried. After she gave her time to get through her cry, she said, "I love you, and I am here for you. You are doing well, and the doctor said you will be fine. I would not leave you if I thought you were not well and not capable of taking care of yourself. I just think you need time to think, and then hopefully you will make wise decisions. I love you, Katheryn."

With a hug and kiss on Katheryn's cheek from Emilia and Rose, they both said their goodbyes and left. Emilia and Rose both believed leaving Katheryn alone to be by herself would help her and she could also make decisions on her own without influence. Emilia and Rose also decided not to tell her that Jonathan had gone home.

After things settled down, Katheryn picked up the blue box and held it for a moment. Then she opened the box and laid the box lid to the side. She looked into the box and smiled. Grand had everything organized. She had put everything in the order they came. Katheryn thanked Grand, took out the first letter, and started reading. She cried, cried more, and thought, *How could I have been such a fool!* She continued to read and cried again and again. Finally, after Katheryn had read the last letter she said out loud, "First thing tomorrow I will try to find Jonathan and tell him. I will beg him to listen to me. Please, God, don't let it be too late."

She got into bed, took her medicine, and planned what she would say to Jonathan the next day. She knew she loved him; she knew he was the one, like Grand said it would be. She just hoped it wasn't too late and her time had run out. She was truly sorry about Ryan, but she knew for sure she loved Jonathan.

The next morning Katheryn took a shower, applied makeup, changed outfits four times, and finally got out the door. She first walked to the lecturing hall to see if he was in class. She looked. He wasn't. She looked everywhere, and she couldn't find him. She decided to go the administration building to find out where he might be. She walked into the administration building and asked the receptionist if Professor O'Conner was lecturing today and if he was, where. The receptionist looked through her computer and found Professor Jonathan O'Conner's name. She looked at his schedule and then looked up at Katheryn and, in a professional tone, said, "Professor O'Conner is no longer on staff as of yesterday."

Katheryn thought, *This couldn't be.* Katheryn asked the receptionist, "Are you sure? Please look again."

The receptionist said, "I will, but the answer will be the same. Yes, this is correct, Professor O'Conner is not on staff as of yesterday. Is there anything else I can help you with?"

Katheryn, stunned, answered the receptionist, "No, thank you." She felt like someone punched her in the stomach. Questions were taking over her brain. *Where is he? Where did he go?* She needed to talk to Grand. She took her cell out and called Grand. Grand didn't answer; it went straight to voice mail. She went back to her apartment and called the hotel to see if Grand was still there. She waited and waited on hold. Finally, a gentleman came back on the phone and said they had checked out. Katheryn sat down on the floor and completely lost it. With makeup running down her cheeks, she sobbed and sobbed. After she had a good cry, she got up, went into the bathroom, washed her face, and then she picked up all of Jonathan's letters with care and neatly put them back in the blue box. She knew she would just have to wait until Grand got home, and then she would call her; surely she had some information about Jonathan.

She waited and cried. Then the process would start all over again. She would wait, and then she would cry.

Katheryn called three times to see if Grand and Rose had got home, and each time when she called, she heard, "No, Miss Katheryn, they haven't returned."

She would hang the phone up and then she would cry because they had not got home yet. She was an absolute mess. She walked into the kitchen to get a bottle of water, and the phone rang. Katheryn jumped. She ran to the phone and answered it. "Hello, Hello, Grand."

Ryan said, "Hate to disappoint you, but this is Ryan. How are you?"

Katheryn answered, "I am fine, Ryan, thank you."

Ryan asked, "Katheryn, are you sick? You sound like you have a cold or something. I hope I am not catching you at a bad time."

Katheryn said to Ryan, "No, I'm not sick, just allergies. I was just expecting a call from my great-grandmother. They left today, and I was just wanting to make sure they got home okay."

Ryan said, "No problem. I will get up with you later. Glad you are okay. Talk to you soon. Take care, Katheryn."

She said, "You too. Bye, Ryan."

Katheryn knew she needed to tell him, but she just could not go there right know. She knew she was not being fair to Ryan, but she just couldn't talk to him at the moment. She dialed Grand again. It rang and rang, then Rose answered, "Hello."

Katheryn took a deep breath and said, "Rose, I am so glad to hear your voice."

Rose asked if there was anything wrong, and Katheryn said, "No, I am fine."

Katheryn asked Rose if she knew anything about Jonathan resigning from Princeton. Rose told her to hang on, she needed to talk to Emilia. Grand came to the phone and said, "Hey, dear, what's up?"

Katheryn asked Grand if she knew anything about Jonathan and did she know where he was. Grand asked, "Did you read his letters?"

Katheryn replied, "Yes, Grand, please tell me. Grand, he is the one."

Emilia smiled and winked at Rose, then she said, "He has moved back home to England. His mother is not well. He left with his father two days ago."

Katheryn said, "Grand, I am going to England."

Emilia said, "Go get your one, dear, I love you."

As soon as they hung up Katheryn started packing. She stopped for a minute and said, "I will never get my master's finished. It is not going to happen."

She called the airlines and booked a flight for the next day out of DC. She finished packing and put everything at the door. Her meds and personal items would go in her backpack. She looked around, made mental notes, and checked things off in her mind. She was ready. She went to bed and set her clock. Katheryn drifted off to sleep thinking about Jonathan.

Chapter 29

Emilia and Rose sat in the Carolina room to have their tea. It was three o'clock in the afternoon. Emilia spoke up and said, "Katheryn should be over the Atlantic somewhere about now, wouldn't you think, Rose?"

Rose placed her cup down on the saucer and looked at Emilia with concern and said, "Yes, I believe she would be. I hope she is not overdoing it, she just got out of the hospital."

Emilia replied, "Oh, I am sure she will be. We checked with the doctor before we said anything.

She just needed to open her eyes and see the big picture."

The two ladies said nothing for a few minutes. They just sat and thought about how they executed a plan to open Katheryn's eyes with a little tough love, and it actually worked. Katheryn read the letters. She chose to look at the episode with Jonathan last year with that silly girl in a different perspective, and now she was on a plane bound for England to find her one. Rose breathed deeply and said, "True love, isn't it beautiful, Emilia!" Emilia smiled and explained to Rose that sometimes it just takes the smallest little push. They both laughed and both agreed it was just a tiny push. Now they waited to hear from Katheryn with anticipation.

Katheryn was asleep and woke when the captain's voice came through the intercom and said they would be arriving at Gatwick International Airport in about thirty minutes. The stewardess handed Katheryn a warm towel, which felt wonderful. She sat upright in her seat and collected her things and her thoughts. She would be near him in less than thirty minutes. She kept wondering if he would still want her after she had been such a brat. Oh, if she had just listened to him, gave him a real chance to explain, but no, she had to run away like a child. Katheryn thought, *I will ask him to forgive me for being so stubborn. I was awful to him.* Katheryn said softly, "I am so sorry, Jonathan, so, so sorry."

The landing was perfect. All she had to do now was get through customs, catch a train, and in a few hours she might see Jonathan.

Customs took forever to get through. Katheryn was feeling her jet lag already. She was tired and wondered if she should just get a hotel in London for a day and rest. Then she could get to Newton Abbot fresh and with a clear head. She headed for the Gatwick express after she got through customs. When she got on the train she laid back and closed her eyes. After she got to London she hailed a cab for the Ritz.

After Katheryn got settled in the hotel she called Grand and Rose to tell them she arrived safely. She was at the Ritz, and tomorrow she would travel to Newton Abbot. After she hung the phone up, she fell across the bed and went sound to sleep. Her medicine timer went off. She woke up, took a pill, and went back to sleep. Katheryn slept from the time she finished her phone call to Grand and Rose until the next morning; she was exhausted.

She woke up the following morning feeling refreshed and ready to start her day. She called room service to bring up coffee and breakfast, took a long hot shower, then ate her breakfast and enjoyed her coffee. She dressed and headed out the door to catch a train.

Katheryn took a cab from the Ritz to Paddington Station where she would take a train to Newton Abbot. She had approximately thirty minutes before she could board. She sat down and just looked around the station. She remembered reading about the station and that it was built in the nineteenth century. She thought, *Still an impressive train station.* Katheryn boarded the train. She felt a little anxiety about seeing Jonathan, then she took a deep breath and told herself everything would be fine. With one change in trains, she should be in Newton Abbot around four o'clock. She had called ahead to get a room at the Union Inn where she had stayed before. The train wreck crept into Katheryn's mind. She prayed, and the thought seemed to dissipate. She knew she should or could have an uneasy feeling traveling on trains again, but she didn't and she contributed that to prayer.

All in all, Katheryn thought she did pretty good time-wise. She arrived in Newton Abbot around three. She went straight to the inn, checked in, and settled in her room. It was the end of January and bitter-cold. She well remembered how cold it was from her visit to Newton Abbot before.

Katheryn stood still. It was like a flood of emotion that hit her. She sat down and gripped the sides of the chair. Katheryn spoke out loud, "I just rode a train twice…no, three times, and it never entered my mind about the accident, except that one small fleeting thought! Other than that, I never thought about it! Thank you, God, for taking care of me." The anxiety started to fade, and Katheryn breathed deeply, knowing she would be fine.

Katheryn tried to find Jonathan's parents' address, but it wasn't in the directory. She decided to go to the hospital to see Dr. O'Conner.

When she arrived at the hospital she went to the information desk and asked if Dr. O'Conner was in today. The girl looked through her schedule and said he was not on today's schedule. She continued to say, "Dr. O'Conner has taken time off due to a family crisis. I am not sure when he will return."

Katheryn was in shock. She turned and walked over to the seating area and sat down. Her mind was raging with questions. *What is going on? Where is the family?* Katheryn knew she needed to find their home. She asked the girl at the desk for their address, but she would not give it to her. Katheryn left. As she walked out the door she said, "I need a car." So she went back to the inn and ordered a car. She asked the guy at the front desk at the inn if he knew Dr. O'Conner, and he said yes. Katheryn said, "Really, you wouldn't happen to know where Dr. O'Conner lives?"

The young man said, "Yes! Right down the street from me."

Katheryn asked if he could write that address down, and he did. The car was delivered. After Katheryn signed the papers and was handed the keys, she slipped into the driver's seat on the wrong side of the car. She prayed, "Lord, this is going to take some getting used to, and I am pretty sure I will need your help." Katheryn looked the car over and noticed right off it was a manual, then she said, "God, I am really going to need you right now!" She knew how to drive a straight drive; Grand had made sure of that when she was twelve. She pushed the clutch in, had her foot on the break, started the car, put her right foot on the gas, and slowly let off her clutch. She eased out onto the street looking both ways, gave the car a little more gas, then changed gears and smiled, saying, "I got this. Thank you, God." After a few miles, Katheryn had no problem driving the car. It was driving on the wrong side of the street that was challenging.

She found the O'Conner house, pulled in the drive, and parked. It was a beautiful home. She went up to the door—nervous but excited—knocked, and waited. The door opened, and a lady said, "May I help you?"

Katheryn said, "Yes, I am looking for Jonathan O'Conner or his father, Dr. O'Conner. They are friends of my family."

The lady said, "I am sorry, they are not here."

Katheryn asked, "Do you know when they will be home?"

The lady said, "I am not sure, they are out of town." Katheryn stood there for a moment then the lady said, "Can I help you with anything else?"

Katheryn knew it was a long shot but went ahead and asked, "Do you know where they might have gone?"

The lady said, "I am not at liberty to disclose that information. Is there anything else I might be able to help you with?"

Katheryn said, "No, thank you."

The lady shut the door, and Katheryn wondered where they were. She drove back to the inn to call Grand.

Emilia heard the phone ring. Rose answered and called out, "It is Katheryn."

Emilia picked up the phone on the table next to her and joined the conversation. Katheryn was saying she could not find the O'Conners, that they were out of town. Emilia said, "Sweetheart, slow down, dear, let me think…well, we know Jonathan's mother is ill. Maybe they have taken her to a specialist!"

Katheryn said, "Oh, Grand, this shouldn't be this hard."

Emilia explained to Katheryn, "Sweetheart, they did not know you were coming! Have you tried to call Jonathan?"

Katheryn said in a defeated tone, "I do not have his number, Grand, and anyway he would have changed phones since he is back in England."

Emilia's voice was steady and, with care, she said, "Just sit tight. Someone will know something, or they will return."

Katheryn replied, "Okay, Grand, I did not even leave my name with the lady that answered the door."

Emilia calmly said, "That is all right, something will turn up. Just be patient, dear. I love you."

Katheryn said, "I love you and Rose. I will call later. Bye"

Chapter 30

Jonathan sat in the waiting room with his family while his mother was in surgery. His father calmly read a journal. His sisters talked quietly amongst themselves. Jonathan was too nervous to read and didn't want to talk. Dr. O'Conner looked over at his son and said, "She will be fine. Dr. Delgrave, your mother's third cousin, is one of the finest surgeons in the country. We have caught this early. There might, and I say might, be a little chemo therapy afterward, but I have the upmost confidence in God and Dr. Delgrave. So steady your nerves, son. Everything will be fine."

Jonathan replied to his father nervously, "I know, Dad, but it is Mum."

Dr. O'Conner put his arm around his son and gave him a hug, and this was just what Jonathan needed. The family continued to wait for the next two hours, then the doctor, still dressed in his surgical clothes, walked up and motioned for them to follow him into another room. Dr. Delgrave shook Dr. O'Conner's hand and said everything went very well, it was contained, and she should make a full recovery. No chemo but a few rounds of radiation to make sure. The family was elated, smiles on every face. They prayed as a family and thanked God for answering their prayers.

After the next couple of days, after seeing how great his mum was doing, Jonathan decided to go back home to take care of the house and things for his dad. Mum would be coming home in the next few days anyway, so he left and took the train home. His sisters would do the same tomorrow, and his father would stay with his Mum.

As Jonathan watched out his window of the train, he thought how things could have turned out different. He prayed a thankful prayer.

Katheryn had been at the inn for almost two weeks, and she could not find out anything. She had been to Jonathan's parents' house three times, with the same answers. She thought, *Maybe I should go back to London.* It was already the second week of February. She had just walked out on her master's not once but twice because of the same guy. She asked herself, *What am I doing? I have given up my life for what, a hope that he might still care. I am going home.* Katheryn packed up, checked out of the inn, turned her car in, and was now at the station waiting on her train for London.

Katheryn just sat in the train station thinking about her life and what in the world was she doing in England. The train from London came in but it was not her train. Katheryn looked at her watch and figured she had about forty-five more minutes.

Jonathan's train rolled into the station at Newton Abbot. He collected his things, and when the train came to a stop, he grabbed his bag and hopped off. He saw a cab and ran to get it. He got in and gave the driver his address. He felt a sense of relief when he saw his parents' home. He got out of the car, paid the driver, got his luggage, and walked inside. He dropped his luggage in the foyer, picked up some mail, and thumbed through it. Ms. Parker, the maid, walked into the foyer and said, "Hello, sir, any news of your mum?"

Jonathan caught her up to speed on his mother's surgery. Ms. Parker was very thankful and pleased. As she started to walk away she turned around and said, "Sir, there was a young lady asking for you while you were gone. She came around several times."

Jonathan laid the mail on the table and asked, "Did she leave a name?"

Ms. Parker said, "Yes, sir, I have it here, just a moment. Yes, here it is. Her name was Katheryn."

Jonathan asked, "Do you know where she is?"

Ms. Parker said, "She mentioned the Union Inn, I believe."

Jonathan grabbed his mother's keys out of the bowl where they all left their keys and ran out the door. He thought, *I can't believe it, she was here!* He got to the inn, parked, and ran in. Jonathan asked the lady at the desk did she have a Katheryn Kensington registered here. The lady said, "Yes, we did, but she checked out this morning, said she was going back to London."

Jonathan asked, "By train?"

The lady said, "Yes."

Jonathan flew out the door, hopped into the car, and drove quickly to the train station. He parked and ran into the station, walked up to the departure board, found the train to London and the platform number. When he got to the platform for the London departure train, he was out of breath. He looked around to see if he could spot her. He looked at his watch and knew he had five minutes before the train left the station. Jonathan thought, she must already be on the train. He started yelling her name as he ran past the cars. "Katheryn! Katheryn! Katheryn!" He saw her. There she was sitting at the window. Jonathan yelled, "Katheryn!" She looked out the window, and there he was, her one. She got up grabbed her backpack and tried to get by the people coming on the train.

"Please let me by, please, he is the one. Please let me pass."

Then she heard, "All aboard."

She begged, "Please let me pass."

She couldn't get off the train, and it was starting to move. Then the train stopped. Katheryn slipped by four more people and was at the door. The door opened, and an elderly couple was being helped on to the train. Katheryn moved out of their way. When the couple was safely onboard, Katheryn stepped off the train into Jonathan's arms. She held him, he held her, and they both cried. Katheryn held him and whispered into his ear, "I love you, Professor Jonathan O'Conner!"

He swung her around and said, "I love you, Katheryn Wardlaw Kensington." He looked down at her and said, "There goes your luggage" as they watched the train leave the station.

Katheryn said, "I do not care, all I need is you."

All that mattered was they were together. Anyone that saw them standing there on the platform would know they were explicitly and undoubtably in love. Jonathan looked down at Katheryn, then he kissed her and she kissed him back with all her love for him. As Jonathan spoke to Katheryn, you could see the love in his eyes. "I am holding on to you. This is forever. This time I will not let you go!"

Katheryn looked up at Jonathan and declared, "You are the one, Professor Jonathan O'Conner. You are definitely stuck with me now. I do not intend on going anywhere!" Katheryn looked at Jonathan and humbly asked, "Will you ever forgive me for being so stubborn and a brat?"

Jonathan pulled her close to him and said, "I love you, Katheryn, and you are the love of my life! There is nothing to forgive."

For the next week they were inseparable, and they were together on Valentine's. He gave her flowers, and they were beautiful.

Katheryn told Grand everything about the train, about Jonathan, and how they were desperately trying to get to each other. Emilia said, "My precious girl, it sounds like a romantic novel! Have you made any plans?"

Katheryn answered, "No, not yet, we are in the moment. Jonathan's mother came home from the hospital two days ago and, Grand, she is such a lovely person."

Emilia, in agreement, said, "Yes, I met her when I was there before. Please give her my regards."

Katheryn said, "I will, Grand, and, Grand, thank you so much."

Emilia asked, "For what, my dear?"

Katheryn, with much love in her heart, said, "For telling me one day I would meet someone that would change my world, and you were right. Jonathan has changed my world. You told me it would happen, and it did!"

Emilia lovingly told her great-granddaughter, "Katheryn, I knew he was the one. You are so welcome, and always know how much I love and adore you."

Katheryn answered straight from her heart, "Grand, I adore you. Talk to you soon, and oh, I forgot to tell you, the entire O'Conner clan said I have to stay with them and not at the inn, so I will move in this evening. Love you. Talk soon, and please tell Rose I send my love."

Emilia hung up her phone with a smile on her face and with the knowledge her girl would be fine knowing she was in love with the one.

Katheryn stayed with the O'Conners through the rest of February and into the first of March. Jonathan pleaded with her to stay until her birthday, March 15. He said he would take her to London for a play. Katheryn caved, but of course it didn't take much. Katheryn told Jonathan, "I can leave from London to go home and get some things settled. I will have to move out of my apartment and then go back to Abbeville to regroup. I do not think I will ever finish my master's, and of course, I have to blame you for that."

Jonathan kissed her and told her she could have his master's, which made her laugh, and then she lovingly hit him on his arm.

Saying goodbye to the O'Conners was hard for Katheryn. She had grown fond of them all, and she loved his mom, his sisters were great, and she loved Dr. O'Conner. It was hard to leave, but she kept saying, "I will be back."

London was absolutely the best birthday Katheryn had ever had. Jonathan thought of everything—the play, the dinner afterward, and the boat ride down the River Thames. She loved him with every fiber of her being, and she knew he loved her because he would tell her in so many ways without saying the words. When Jonathan did say the words I love you, he would look deep into her eyes and tell her, and he would always say, "I will love you forever, my precious Katheryn."

This impending separation would be unbearable for both. They promised each other not to talk about her leaving and to spend every moment together happy. They sat together on the sofa in their suite enjoying a glass of wine the evening before Katheryn was to leave. Jonathan looked at Katheryn and said, "I did not think I could ever love someone as much as I love you"

Katheryn's eyes filled with tears. She softly picked up Jonathan's hand and kissed it. Katheryn whispered, "How can I leave you?" Jonathan put his arms around her, and they just held each until morning.

They woke up in each other's arms. Today she would leave. They got ready, packed, and left for the airport. When they got to the airport Katheryn checked in, then they walked to her gate. She had approximately forty minutes before she had to board. They sat together holding hands. They made plans. She would come back after she took care of her apartment and checked in on Grand. Katheryn heard the attendant call her flight number. She looked at Jonathan. They got up, then Jonathan kissed her and whispered in her ear, "We will be together soon, love."

Tears filled Katheryn's eyes. Katheryn walked to the gate. She was next in line. She turned and kissed Jonathan and said, "We will not say goodbye, we will say I will see you soon. So I will see you soon, love."

Then Jonathan answered, "I will see you soon, love."

Katheryn turned, still holding his hand until she could hold it no longer, then walked through the gate. When she sat down in her seat on the plane the tears rolled down her face; she was the happiest and saddest she had ever been in her life all at the same time.

Chapter 31

It was eight o'clock in the morning, and Katheryn was almost finished cleaning out her apartment. Everything was ready and packed for the movers to pick up and take back to South Carolina for storage. She had an ache in her heart for Jonathan; she had missed him every second since she last saw him at the London airport. They had talked, but it just wasn't the same as being together. She longed for his touch and especially his hugs.

Katheryn would leave for home after the movers left today. There was a knock at the door. Katheryn answered and let the movers in. Katheryn figured she would be leaving in a couple of hours, but in reality, four hours later she locked the door to her apartment for the last time and left for home.

As Katheryn drove home, she thought about Ryan Wardlaw as she passed through Virginia. Katheryn remembered their last conversation. She had called him from England to tell him she was still in love with someone else. Ryan was very sweet about the news and wished her all the luck in the world, but Katheryn thought it was a little too easy reaction on his part and he probably hated her.

As Katheryn passed through North Carolina it was evening. The ride had been easy and peaceful. She knew she would get in late, but she had already talked to Grand and she was aware of the time she would arrive.

Katheryn woke up in her bedroom at Grand's the next morning. She had got in really late. Grand and Rose got up and told her they loved her, and everyone went back to bed. Katheryn laid in the bed with the sun already shining in. She looked to see what time is was; her watch said nine forty-five. Katheryn thought, *I have almost slept to ten o'clock!*

She got up, showered, and got ready, then she went downstairs to see Grand and Rose. She could still smell the remnants of breakfast and was hoping there was something left. Katheryn found Grand and Rose in the Carolina room reading the paper and still having coffee. Katheryn called out to Grand and Rose, "Good morning, ladies."

Grand and Rose both at the same time said, "Good morning to you!"

Grand told Katheryn to please sit and tell her all the news from London. Katheryn said, "I will as soon as I get something eat. I am starving." Grand called her maid and asked her to bring Katheryn a full breakfast.

After Katheryn ate her breakfast, she gave a play-by-play account of what happened in England to Grand and Rose. They both thought it was the most romantic story they had ever heard. Then the questions started. "When will you see each other again? Is he coming here? Are you going back there?"

Katheryn just smiled and said, "I am home for a while, then I will go back to England to spend time with Jonathan. We have made no specific plans at the moment, and I have got to figure out how I am going to finish my master's."

Emilia looked at Katheryn with the sweetest smile and said, "Everything will work out, my dear, then we will plan the most beautiful wedding Abbeville has ever seen."

Katheryn smiled at the thought and said, "Well, marriage has not been mentioned yet, Grand. I am just enjoying being in love at the moment."

Emilia exclaimed, "This is so exciting!"

All three laughed, cried, and laughed again until lunch was served. Katheryn felt so much love from these two women. For her entire life they had always been there for her, and she loved them dearly.

The days flew by so quickly; it had almost been two weeks since Katheryn came home to Grand's. She had booked her flight for England and would leave in three days. Jonathan and Katheryn talked constantly, and she looked forward to their calls, but every time she hung up she missed him more. Jonathan kept telling her their phone bills will put them in the poor house. It was really expensive, but

Katheryn didn't care. She had to hear the sound of his voice.

Emilia called for Katheryn to hurry. They were going to the club for dinner, and she did not want to be late for their reservation. Katheryn hurried down the stairs and out the door to the car. They were all looking forward to eating at the club tonight because they were serving lobster and steak. They got to the club with time to spare, and the maître d' seated them as soon as they walked through the door. It was a lovely restaurant, and Katheryn always enjoyed coming here with Grand. As the waiter filled their water glasses Emilia clasped her chest, then there was an array of activity. As Katheryn held her in her arms she pleaded, "Grand, please hang in there. The ambulance will be here soon."

Emilia was rushed to the hospital. Katheryn and Rose followed in the car. Their driver pulled up to the emergency room. Rose and Katheryn were in a dead run to get to Emilia. They were asked to take a seat after being told the doctors was assessing the patient. Katheryn and Rose sat in the waiting room for what seemed hours. Finally, someone came and told them that she was taken to ICU on the heart floor and they could go to the waiting room on that particular floor. Katheryn asked, "Do you know what is wrong with her?"

The nurse said, "The doctor will talk to you after you check in to the ICU waiting room." Katheryn and Rose immediately went to look for the ICU waiting room. They found it and checked in.

They waited for another hour, and finally the doctor came to talk to them. Katheryn and Rose both knew the doctor, and he knew them; he had taken care of Emilia forever. Dr. Barnet walked up and said, "Hello, Katheryn, Rose." He sat down to talk with them and said, "I know you are worried, but I think she will be fine. She has an irregular heartbeat, but we can regulate that with a pacemaker implant, which we have scheduled for tomorrow. She is fine right now and being monitored. You should go home and get some rest and come back tomorrow. The surgery is set for nine o'clock tomorrow morning. She is resting right now, and of course we have her sedated."

Katheryn said, "Thank you, Dr. Barnet. We will be here tomorrow morning."

Katheryn and Rose went home to get some rest and to pack somethings for Emilia to take tomorrow.

After they got home Katheryn and Rose went to the kitchen to make something light to eat. As they were sitting at the island in the kitchen trying to eat a sandwich, Katheryn looked at Rose and said, "I can't go to England until I know Grand is fine and recovered."

Rose understood and tried to convey that to Katheryn by saying, "She will be fine I am sure, but I also know you wouldn't want to leave under the current circumstances." Rose patted Katheryn's hand, then put her arm around her and said, "I love you, child."

Katheryn hugged Rose and said, "I love you too."

Rose told Katheryn, "We really need to get some rest, sweetheart, we have to be at the hospital very early."

The next morning Katheryn and Rose were at the hospital at eight. They still could not see her. So they sat and waited. Katheryn looked at her watch and it was eleven o'clock and they hadn't heard anything. She and Rose were starting to get worried. Katheryn looked down the hall and saw Dr. Barnet coming. They were both anxious. Dr. Barnet smiled at Katheryn and Rose. He then said, "She did fine. She is doing great. She went through the procedure like a champ. We will keep her here for a few days then she can go home."

Katheryn asked, "When can we see her?"

Dr. Barnett said, "She will be asleep for a while. Go and get something to eat 'cause I am sure you haven't eaten, and when you come back you should be able to visit with her for a little while."

Katheryn and Rose were so relieved and thankful. They went to the cafeteria to eat and didn't realize they were so hungry until they walked in and smelled the burgers cooking. They ate and went back upstairs to see Emilia.

Katheryn and Rose walked quietly into Emilia's room. She was resting, they thought, until they heard Emilia say, "Where have you two been?"

Katheryn said, "Here, they would not let us in until now. How do you feel, Grand?"

Emilia answered Katheryn, "I think I feel fine. I am pretty sure. Guess this pacemaker will keep me from embarrassing myself at the club. That must have been awful." Katheryn and Rose played it down, telling Emilia that it was not bad at all. Emilia said, "I know it was, girls."

Rose looked at Katheryn and said, "Well, we tried. Yes, it was awful."

Katheryn called Jonathan and let him know what was going on. She said she was heartbroken because she would not be able to come as planned, but she needed to stay with Grand. Jonathan totally understood with what he had been through with his mother. Katheryn asked, "How is your mom doing?"

Jonathan answered, "She is doing great, practically back to normal."

Katheryn said, "Oh, Jonathan, that is wonderful. Please tell her I send my best." He said he would and then told Katheryn how much he missed her and loved her. Katheryn said, "I love you, and I will see you soon."

After Katheryn ended her phone call with Jonathan, she went back to Grand's room to sit with her. She found Grand sitting up in the bed reading the *Abbeville News*. Katheryn thought, *She is on the mend.* Grand told Katheryn she sent Rose to the hospital store to get a few things, and when she gets back she wanted them both to go home to rest. Then she said, "But only after you tell me all about Jonathan."

Katheryn laughed and said to Grand, "He sends his love to you. His mother is doing great, and he totally understands I have to delay my trip."

Grand said, "You should go, my dear, I am fine!"

Katheryn explicitly answered her great-grandmother with "I am not going at this time, and that is the end of this particular conversation. I am staying put for now! Now what can I do for you?"

Grand answered, "Okay, go home and get some rest. I am fine."

Rose returned from the hospital store with Emilia's items and laid them within Emilia's reach. Katheryn bent over and gave Emilia a kiss on her cheek and said, "I love you, and I will see you in the morning."

Emilia smiled and told her she loved her too, then she said, "Now you two scoot, go home and get some rest! I will see you tomorrow."

Katheryn and Rose left the hospital thanking God for taking care of Grand. All three women had a huge scare in the last forty-eight hours. Katheryn was more exhausted than she thought; she looked forward to a restful night's sleep.

Chapter 32

Jonathan had a few more strings to tie up on his research, and then he would be ready to leave. He had booked his ticket for Atlanta, Georgia, and would leave tomorrow morning. He had not told Katheryn he was coming; he wanted it to be a surprise. He had a meeting at four this afternoon, and then he would be ready to leave with everything in order.

The next morning, Jonathan boarded his plane bound for the United States. He smiled every time he thought of what Katheryn's reaction would be when she saw him. He loved her with his entire heart and soul and had really loved her long before she told him she love him.

Jonathan thought about their journey, his and Katheryn's from the time he knew who she was until now. He was looking forward to a wonderful future with her and hopefully no more separations. He looked down at his watch and calculated what time he would land taking in the time difference, then how long it would take him to get to Katheryn. He was landing in Atlanta, Georgia, then he would have to rent a car and drive to Abbeville, South Carolina, which should take around three hours. Jonathan thought he should be at Katheryn's around five in the afternoon, eastern standard time. He laid back in his seat and closed his eyes to get some sleep because this was going to be a long day.

While Jonathan was in the air traveling to see Katheryn, she was asleep. She awakened at eight that morning, got up and dressed, and went downstairs to check on Grand to make sure she wasn't overdoing it since she came home from the hospital. She found Grand in the dining room on the phone talking to someone about installing an elevator. Emilia had said to Katheryn the night before that one day the steps might be too much for her. Katheryn actually thought it was a great idea. The house had a perfect place to install it; they could put it in two stacked closets that were large enough to accommodate an elevator. Katheryn thought this would be wonderful for Grand because it gave her the ability to always stay in her own suite of rooms upstairs.

While Grand was still talking to the elevator company, Katheryn filled her plate with eggs, bacon, fruit, grits, and a wonderful warm biscuit from the breakfast buffet placed on the side board in the dining room. She sat down to eat a scrumptious breakfast. She was lathering butter and jam on her biscuit when Grand said in a dry tone, "Hungry, dear?"

Katheryn announced, "Grand, I am starved, and this is so good! I looked forward to Wednesdays and Sundays when we have the full breakfast!"

Emilia smiled at her lovely Katheryn and said, "You are always a delight."

After breakfast Katheryn took Grand in for her checkup with the cardiologist, and everything checked out beautifully. Then they went to the flower market. It was April and the flowers coming into the market were so pretty and the fragrances were almost overwhelming. This was something Katheryn always enjoyed doing with Grand. They were both still full from their breakfast, so they decided just to stop in at the tea house for a nice cup of tea.

After tea, Grand was a little tired, so they went back to the house for her to rest. Grand was excited about the fact she could put an elevator in with no structural problems and couldn't wait for them to start. Katheryn told Grand she should rest and then they would play a game of scrabble, another activity they both enjoyed doing together.

While Grand was taking a nap, Katheryn decided to call Jonathan, but the call would not go through. She thought that was odd and she would try later. She went into the study and started working on her research. She had uncovered several things about the Delgraves and was getting excited about some new leads. She was looking forward to when she went back to England, to her Jonathan, and to follow up on her leads and hopefully uncover some new information on the lost ring.

Katheryn had been working for several hours, she decided to stop for a moment and check on Grand. She found Grand in the Carolina room reading. She went up to her and gave her a kiss on her cheek and asked, "What are you reading, Grand?" Emilia closed her book as Katheryn protested, "Please don't stop because of me!"

Emilia smiled at her great granddaughter and said, "I am ready to take a break, my dear."

Katheryn looked at the time, and it was four thirty. Then she asked Grand what time were they eating supper. Emilia told her at five or so. Katheryn said, "Good, I am getting a little hungry, and when will Rose be back from visiting her sister?"

Emilia answered, "Tomorrow."

The doorbell rang, and Katheryn said, "Wonder who that could be?"

Emilia said, "Not sure, dear." But Emilia knew who was at the door. Katheryn and Emilia waited for Renee to answer the door.

Katheryn heard Renee say, "Right through here, sir. Yes, you are welcome."

She looked at Emilia with a puzzled look on her face, and then she heard his voice say in a very distinct English accent, "Hello, ladies."

Katheryn was so taken back she couldn't speak, and Emilia smiled and said, "Welcome, Jonathan."

Katheryn jumped up, through her arms around his neck. He kissed her with such sweetness, and then she cried. Jonathan held her and with a consoling voice, saying, "There...there, my love."

Then he looked at Emilia smiling and winked at her. Katheryn said, "You must be exhausted, how did you get here? Where did you fly into? Are you hungry? Oh, Jonathan, I am so happy to see you."

Jonathan answered, "Yes, rented car, Atlanta, yes, I am hungry."

He laughed, and then he kissed her again. Emilia looked on the two with such fondness and said, "Well, my dear Jonathan, you have arrived just at the right time."

They all three went into the dining room. Emilia asked for another place setting for the table.

They had a wonderful meal together; they laughed, Emilia toasted, Jonathan toasted, and Katheryn laughed at the two. Katheryn thought, as she looked at two of the most important people in her life, how happy and thankful she was.

After supper, Emilia went on up to her room. Katheryn got Jonathan settled in his room. He dropped on the bed and said, "I could sleep forever."

Katheryn sat beside him and said, "You rest, you have had a long day." Before she could say I love you, he was asleep. She covered him up with a blanket, kissed him on his forehead, and tiptoed out the door.

Jonathan was up early. He showered, shaved, and came out of his room at seven. He smelled coffee coming up from downstairs and wondered if he might get a cup of tea. When he walked into the kitchen, Charlotte, the cook, asked, "Can I help you, sir?"

Jonathan said, "Yes, may I trouble you for a cup of tea?"

Charlotte answered, "Yes, sir, I will bring it out to you. Maybe in the Carolina room?"

Jonathan smiled and said, "That would be excellent." He walked into the Carolina room to find Emilia already there having a cup of coffee. Jonathan said, "Good morning."

Emilia smiled and said, "Come and join me, Jonathan. Shall I call for you some coffee?"

Jonathan told Emilia he had already asked for tea and thanked her. Charlotte walked in with a tray with Jonathan's tea and some pastries. Jonathan was delighted. After he poured his tea and added cream, he turned to Emilia and said, "I have it."

Emilia was stunned and said, "Really?"

Katheryn walked into the room, and Jonathan stood up. She kissed him and said, "Good morning, did you sleep well?"

Jonathan smiled at her and said, "Yes, just like a baby."

Katheryn poured herself a coffee and grabbed a pastry. She just smiled at him, and he just smiled at her. Emilia smiled at them and was thankful her girl was in love with a fine young man.

Jonathan looked at his love and said, "Katheryn, I would like for you to take a little trip with me.

Don't ask, it is a surprise! We will stay overnight." He reiterated, "Don't ask."

Katheryn said, "Okay, when do we leave?"

Jonathan answered, "Today, if we can."

Emilia said, "Go, Rose is coming back today. In fact she will be here this morning, so go."

Jonathan and Katheryn left around noon. He had it all planned out. Katheryn would start asking questions, but Jonathan kept saying it was a surprise. The trip would take about six or seven hours. Jonathan had booked a suite at a bed-and-breakfast last week. When they arrived at the bed-and-breakfast, Katheryn told Jonathan it was absolutely beautiful. It was late evening so they could not see all the grounds, but Jonathan said that would be a treat in the morning. The house was lit up like a Christmas tree with white lights everywhere; it looked like a wonderland to Katheryn. Jonathan checked them in, and they went to their suite. Katheryn thought the entire place was magical and wonderfully quaint. They ate dinner in the grand dining room. The food was delicious. After dinner they took a carriage ride around the property.

Katheryn loved every minute, and she was enjoying herself so much she stopped asking what, why, and where they were going.

They went back to their rooms and settled in for the evening. Jonathan had a bottle of chilled wine and a selection of cheeses brought to their suite. Katheryn looked at Jonathan and said, "What a wonderful evening. You keep surprising me. I am truly spoiled now." Jonathan told Katheryn he just wanted to get away with her and have her all by himself. They held each other until wee hours of the morning, not even wanting to let go of each other to sleep.

They both slept in the next morning. Jonathan got up first and ordered in coffee and tea with pastries. They had missed breakfast, which was fine with both of them. Katheryn came out of her room as soon as she smelled the coffee. They both said at the same time, "Good morning, love." They smiled lovingly at each other then they embraced and didn't want to let go. Jonathan explained to Katheryn that he had something special to show her. They reluctantly parted to get ready for the day. When they stepped outside, the grounds took Katheryn's breath away; it was absolutely beautiful. The azaleas were in bloom; there were flowers everywhere. Jonathan looked at Katheryn and said, "This place is really very pretty!" Katheryn couldn't think of a word that would do it justice, so she said plainly, "It is gorgeous!"

As they rode a short way in the car, Katheryn started asking questions again. Jonathan told her to be patient. Jonathan parked at what looked like a farm. He helped Katheryn out of the car, and they walked a short distance to a beautiful valley of wild flowers. Jonathan took Katheryn's hand and led her down a little path, and then he stopped. Jonathan turned and looked at the love of his life, took both of her hands in his, and said, "I love you, Katheryn Wardlaw Kensington, with all my heart and soul." Then Jonathan got down on one knee. He took this little box out of his pocket, opened it up, and there was a beautiful ruby ring in it. Then he asked, "Katheryn Wardlaw Kensington, will you marry me?"

Katheryn looked down at her love and said, "Yes, Jonathan, I will marry you! Yes, yes!"

Jonathan stood up and put the beautiful ruby ring on Katheryn's finger. Katheryn instantly noticed the ring was an antique. She looked at Jonathan and then she looked back at the ring then she asked, "This couldn't be the ring?"

He answered, "Yes, it could and it is."

Katheryn asked, "How did you ever find it? Oh, Jonathan, it is exquisite. It is absolutely beautiful."

Jonathan asked Katheryn if she knew where she was. She looked around, then she looked at him and asked, "Are we in the valley where the wildflowers grow? Oh my gosh, we are here! Jonathan! This is the place, this is where William proposed to Catriona and gave her this very ring!" Katheryn could not believe Jonathan had found the ring, much less the special valley where the wild flowers grow. She looked at him and said, "I will love you forever and ever. Thank you for this. It is unbelievable!" Jonathan took her into his arms, kissed her, and knew he had, with Emilia's help, done well.

As they drove back to South Carolina, Katheryn pleaded with Jonathan to tell her how he discovered her beautiful family ring. Jonathan started the story with "If I tell you, you have to promise to still marry me. Okay?"

Katheryn said, "I promise."

Jonathan said, "I will hold you to that promise, Katheryn!"

Jonathan started the story. "When you told me the first time about the name Delgrave, I thought that name was familiar. When my mum was in the hospital, her third cousin, Dr. Delgrave, took care of her. After you left I went to see Dr. Delgrave and told him your story and about the ring. Dr. Delgrave told me his mum had a ring like I described, so I went to see her. She is a very gracious lady. After I told her the entire story, she got up and went to a large cabinet. She unlocked the cabinet and took out a small box. She walked over to me and handed me the box and asked, 'Is this the ring?' I opened the box, and it was exactly how Emilia described it. Mrs. Delgrave told me to take it home where it belonged. I offered to pay her, but she insisted that I bring it to you."

Katheryn said, "Wow! It is unbelievable. I cannot believe you actually found it and she gave it to you, Jonathan. She actually gave it to you!"

Jonathan explained to Katheryn, "Your Grand helped tremendously. She had the description from stories handed down through the generations, and it is beautiful."

Katheryn said, "I cannot wait to show Grand." Jonathan couldn't tell Katheryn that he had already shown it to Emilia. Katheryn said to Jonathan, "I don't think I could be any happier than I am today. I love you so much, Professor Jonathan O'Conner."

Jonathan reached for Katheryn's hand brought it to his lips and kissed it, then replied, "You are the love of my life, Katheryn Wardlaw Kensington!"

Epilogue

On April 5, 1997, Katheryn Wardlaw Kensington and Dr. Jonathan Alexander O'Conner III were married in Abbeville, South Carolina, in an intimate ceremony with family and close friends.

The bride's great-grandmother, Mrs. Emilia Wardlaw Kensington, gave her away. The groom's father, Dr. Jonathan Alexander O'Conner II, was his best man. The marriage took place at the bride's great-grandmother's home in the garden. The couple honeymooned in Scotland and now reside in London, England, where the groom is employed and the bride will continue to work on her masters!

Love is patient, love is kind. It does not envy, it does not boast, it is not proud. It is not rude, it is not self-seeking. It is not easily angered, it keeps no record of wrongs. Love does not delight in evil but rejoices with the truth. It always protects, always trusts, always hopes, always perseveres. (1 Corinthians 13:4–7 NIV)

About the Author

Patricia Lewis-Burrell is an author of Christian fiction romantic novels with a touch of history woven in through the pages of each book she writes. She is from Upstate South Carolina and now resides on the coast of South Carolina with her sidekick, Piper, a West Highland terrier. Traveling and seeing the world has, and still is, one of her passions as well as art, photography, and writing. She says the wander-lust in her cannot be satisfied; she is always wanting to explore new places on our beautiful planet.

CPSIA information can be obtained
at www.ICGtesting.com
Printed in the USA
LVHW040347140722
723387LV00002B/142